HENRY'S GIFT

TURPA FORTUNA NON EST DOMINA MEA

HENRY'S GIFT
The Magic Eye

Written by David Worsick

Illustrations by Joyce Harris

Three Dimensional Images by Bohdan Petyhyrycz, Jr.

Andrews and McMeel
A Universal Press Syndicate Company
Kansas City

CREDITS

Writer: David F. Worsick

Illustrator: Joyce Harris

3D Creators

Art Director: Bohdan Petyhyrycz

Project Manager: Peter Ciavarella

Software Development:
Olaf Schroeder
Stuart May

Modelers:
Pat Keenan
Gwen Hughes

3D Image Creation:
Adelina Banks
Ferdinand Csaky
Brent Gusdal
Dave Hunter
Ava Lazzarotto
Eric Trouillot
Yvan Trouillot

Jacket Design: Ferdinand Csaky
Story Editor: Tony King

And thanks to the staff of Digi-Rule Inc.

Special thanks to Tom Baccei of N.E. Thing Enterprises
and Mark Gregorek of Blue Moon Licensing.

HENRY'S GIFT: THE MAGIC EYE
Copyright © 1994 by Digi-Rule Inc.
All rights reserved. Printed in the United States of America.
Magic Eye is a TM of N.E. Thing Enterprises.
No part of this book may be used or reproduced in any manner whatsoever without written permission
except in the case of reprints in the context of reviews.
For information write Andrews and McMeel, a Universal Press Syndicate Company, 4900 Main Street, Kansas City, Missouri 64112.

ISBN: 0-8362-7019-3

Library of Congress Catalog Card Number: 94-79599

Attention: Schools and Businesses

Andrews and McMeel books are available at quantity discounts with bulk purchase for educational, business, or sales promotional use.
For information write to: Special Sales Department, Andrews and McMeel, 4900 Main Street, Kansas City, Missouri 64112.

The Baron of Veldran scratched the graying hairs on his head as he studied his adopted son, his only child. Henry sat, staring blankly out the window overlooking the low hills of this small barony. Was he just daydreaming? Or did he see something in the puffs of cloud above the stony fields of wild flowers and sheep?

The Baron had long ago given up trying to understand the boy's visions. Henry saw things no one else could. When he gazed at the patterns within the tapestries, the random swirls of the morning fog, or the rhythmic flow of the grain fields, he caught glimpses of battling warriors or visions of ghostly knights. The Baron studied the tapestry on the wall. Henry claimed this fabric consistently gave him the same vision. Yet the decoration of flowers in that artwork could not possibly resemble a mounted knight.

A blessing from angels or a curse from demons, the Baron felt only the fates could say. Even though nobody else saw these visions, no one doubted them. Henry's descriptions were too vivid. So Henry wasn't mad; cursed by the fates perhaps, but not mad.

The fates might also have a say in these gifts, he thought, looking over the presents beside Henry. A sickly boy most of his life, Henry became a man this day solely because of his years, not for any deed. Yet the gifts were for a traveler: a heavy riding coat from his mother, a riding saddle from the knights of the barony, a plain fighter's dagger from Byron, Henry's closest friend and a knight-in-training.

"Are these omens, Henry?"

The boy's head snapped away from the window at the sound of his name. The Baron smiled at his bemused face: just daydreaming today. "I wonder if these gifts are omens, Henry." He waved a hand in the direction of Nadia.

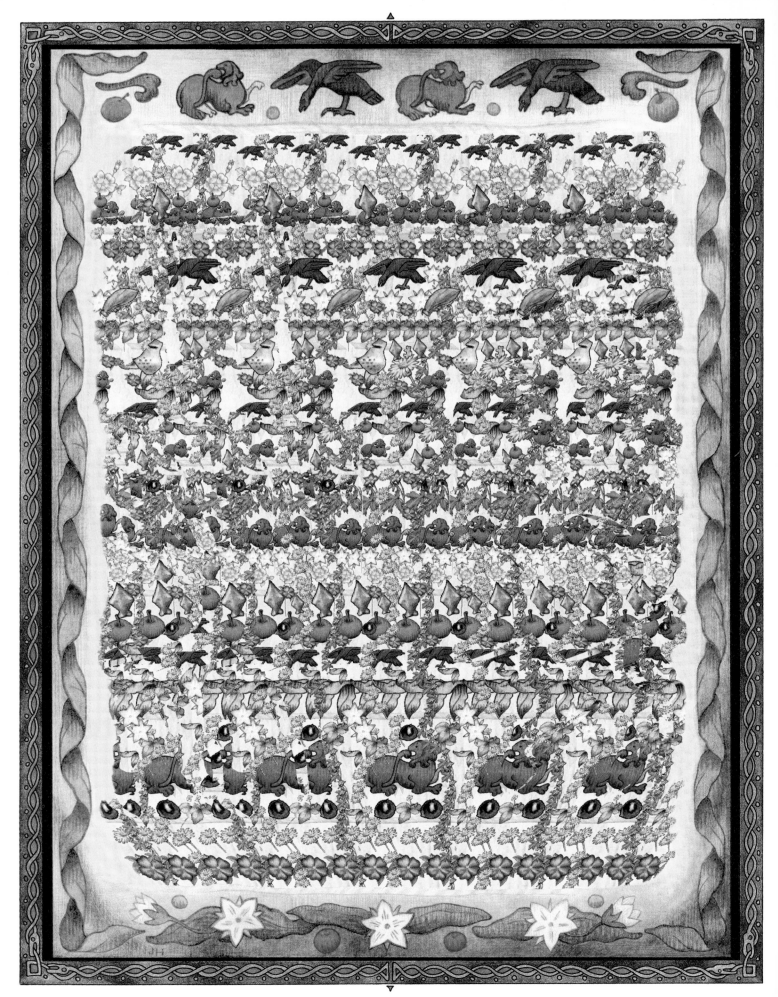

"Even the shepherd's daughter gave you something for traveling."

"This?" Henry lifted the warm woolen sweater, patterned with the same brown shade as the long hair cascading over the shoulders of the girl who knitted it.

"Surely that's too warm to wear reading books by the fire."

Henry's pale face reddened. Mastering books and numbers had been his son's escape from a childhood of illness. Only in the last years had Henry grown strong enough to learn to ride, and still he could not leave the safe trails in the nearby forest.

The Baron reached beside his platter and closed his hands around his gift. He stopped. For a fleeting moment, he argued with himself over giving it. He spoke quietly, but all heads turned in his direction. "If a man can't keep his word to himself, how can he keep it for anyone else!"

"Pardon me, Father?" Henry's head tilted to one side.

"I made a promise to myself on the day we found you in the courtyard, Henry."

"A promise?"

"Whoever left you to us, left something else in the basket. It's as much a mystery as your parentage, and I vowed you should have it when you became a man." He walked over and handed an ancient parchment scroll to Henry. "This is my gift to you, my son."

Still looking puzzled, Henry accepted the scroll and untied the silk knot. The maidservant cleared the table and Henry laid the parchment out flat. Everyone but Nadia leaned over the table to examine the jumble of Latin words inscribed over runes, the alphabet of the legendary Vikings.

"I have studied that parchment with many priests and scholars. None could decipher it. But we always felt there was something important, perhaps even mystical, about it." The boy's eyes widened and he returned his attention to the parchment.

Henry recognized the letter forms, but they seemed to spell only incoherent, unpronounceable words. He could read several languages, and none of these were in the parchment. He was about to declare it gibberish when an image appeared among the letters, a map of the foothills in the kingdom to the east.

A shiver ran down Henry's back. The country shown was a land of wealthy plains and mine-peppered mountains, ruled by a tyrant. Baron Vladimir had stolen its crown from the true royal family. His son now sat on the throne.

"The Necromancer," Henry muttered.

People whispered that King Ivan used the black arts to raise ghosts to spy on his lands. The hills of those lands were haunted by sudden death and lingering madness.

According to this map, something else was hidden in the hills.

"Ivan?" the Baron asked. "What has that murderous tyrant to do with this?"

Henry's hands nervously traced the outline of the map on the parchment. "It's a map. Can't you see? There's something hidden there."

"What? In Ivan's cursed hills?"

Henry nodded, still staring at the parchment.

"Well, what is it, son? I don't see anything."

"I don't really know." Henry shook his head.

For the first time since Henry had spread the parchment on the table, Nadia leaned over to look.

"Perhaps," she said, "I know someone who can help."

The next day, after Henry tallied the number and recorded the worth of new barrels of honey and bales of wool, he met Nadia at the castle gates. He helped her onto his horse, and she easily balanced sideways behind him. As they rode, she directed him toward the forest edge and the mud plaster cottage of an old woman.

Nadia warmly greeted the old woman, who led both of them into her hovel. When Henry showed the woman the mysterious parchment, she fixed her eyes upon it and sighed.

"It's the parchment, in front of me, the actual parchment. I had only heard stories. And now I can actually look upon it. Sit. The legend! I'll tell you the legend.

"When young I was and training in the lore of herbs, the kingdom to the east was my home. Our beloved ruler was King Sigismund the Third, with his noble son, Frederick the Fair.

"Sigismund went south with a large army, to defend our borders from bandit raids. Yet these were not bandits at all, but a secret army of mercenaries. They came from the east, the south, and even the west. In great numbers they attacked. Poor King Sigismund was slain. Blinded and grief-stricken we were, totally helpless without an army."

As he listened, Henry noticed Nadia staring at the woman's gnarled hands, leaning close to her as if to make each spoken word as loud as possible.

"Unwary were we. One of our own dukes had betrayed us. He made treacherous alliances with some of the neighboring kingdoms, even the khan of the horsemen to the east. That duke, Vladimir, may demons drag him through a crack in the earth, was a giant of a man. With a greed to match his size."

The old woman fingered the parchment, holding it upside down.

"He raised a small army to attack one of our castles on the northern frontier. At his own father's funeral, Frederick learned of the siege. What was left of the garrisons he gathered and rode out to the stricken castle. But then, Duke Vladimir's army and the eastern horsemen ambushed Frederick. They destroyed him and his army. The castle fell, and so did all who resisted.

"But the final victory was too late for that monster Vladimir. In that battle, he also died."

As she spoke, Henry gazed out the doorway at the distant wheat fields, watching the wind dance with the stalks of grain. He let the swaying heads of wheat frame his mind's pictures of the woman's story.

"Vladimir's runt of a son, Ivan, took over the throne when he was a pup. We had called him Ivan, the Reader of Dark Books, and, guided by his mother's vile knowledge, he became the Necromancer.

"The treasury and royal crowns had been hidden away by brave loyalists. Ivan's horsemen searched everywhere for that treasure, sweeping through the land like a plague, but in vain. The treasury remained hidden.

"Servants, closer to that cursed family than I, claimed the Witch would descend to her dungeon to weave horrifying spells. For all her blasphemy, she had not found the treasure of our wretched kingdom.

"About a dozen years after the Great Betrayal and a week after the Witch had died, I was in the duke's castle delivering rare herbs. Servants told me this story. After spending an entire night and day submerged in the dark secrets of her dungeon, the old Witch had taken to bed. Outside howled the wind, and a thick mist flowed out of the forest to storm the castle walls. The head of the guards ran from the ramparts to warn that they were being besieged by an unearthly army of dark, shadowy forms. The Witch only smiled and said 'They are ready. They have found it and will never let it go. But it's too late. I have one more spell to cast. I can guard it for Ivan.'"

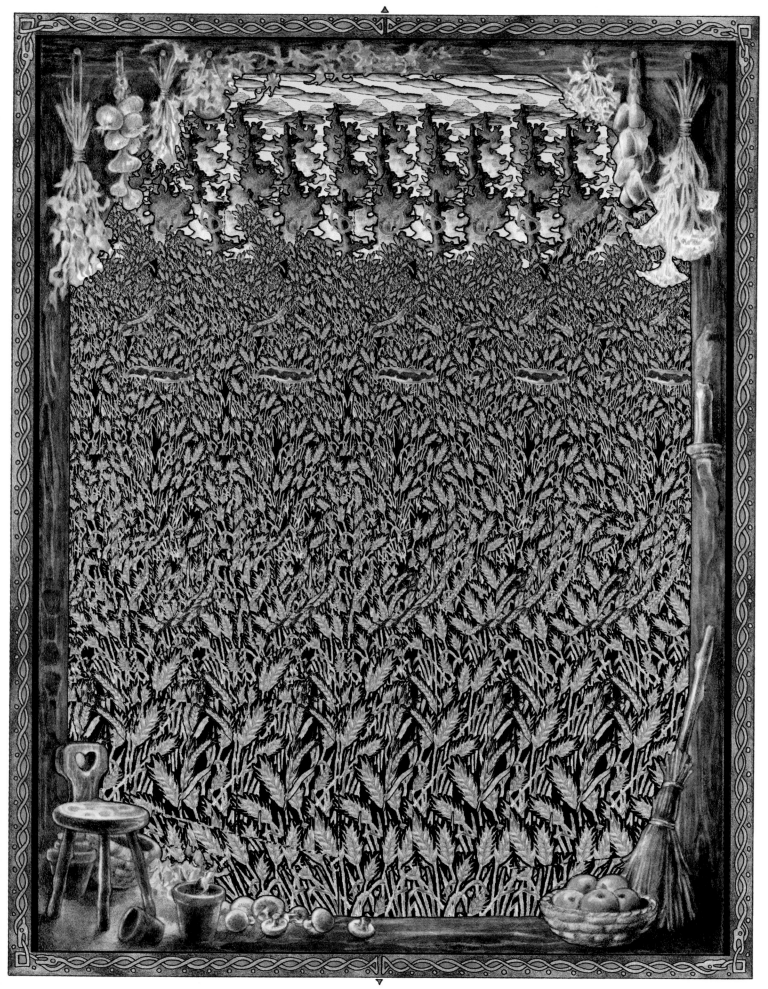

At those words, Henry saw a strange vision forming in the wind-blown rows of wheat. Henry lost the vision after a few moments and shook off his foreboding. The old woman had stopped and stared at him, with a puzzled look on her face. He said, "I'm sorry. I let my mind drift away."

The old woman continued, watching him closely.

"There was a sudden burst of smoke at the foot of the Witch's bed. The guard fled the chamber, screaming about a horrible ogre. When more soldiers arrived, the Witch was alone, dead, and smiling more peacefully than she deserved. The mist and the dark army had also disappeared from the castle walls. A sealed message sat by the Witch's bed addressed to her son, Ivan. He was far away in the royal palace on the throne he had stolen."

She paused to remember, clasping her hands.

"One guard claimed to have seen some of this message, read over Ivan's shoulder. What he saw was this strange prophesy: 'Ivan must be first to gain the treasure, or else fall as quickly once as his father did twice.'"

The old woman stopped talking. Henry looked at her for an explanation, but she only shrugged her shoulders and continued.

"People say the hills where Vladimir and Frederick battled are haunted by an army eternally cheated of death. Those who had gone to search for Frederick's treasure were never able to tell what they had seen, for they were either found gibbering with madness or mute with death.

"But, there are some, loyal to our beloved Frederick, who claim there is a magical parchment. Whoever can read it will be immune to such a terrible fate and shall restore virtue to the kingdom and free the people. I believe you have that very parchment. If you can find someone who can read its magic, you will know more than I."

"You cannot read it?"

"No." The old woman shook her head slowly.

Henry sat in silence for a few seconds while Nadia thanked the old woman. He took Nadia's hand and stepped into the doorway. He stopped and turned. "One more thing. Do you know any place where I can find a plant called the Mandrake?"

The old woman looked at him wide-eyed. "Yes." She leaned over to him and whispered directions to a secret path.

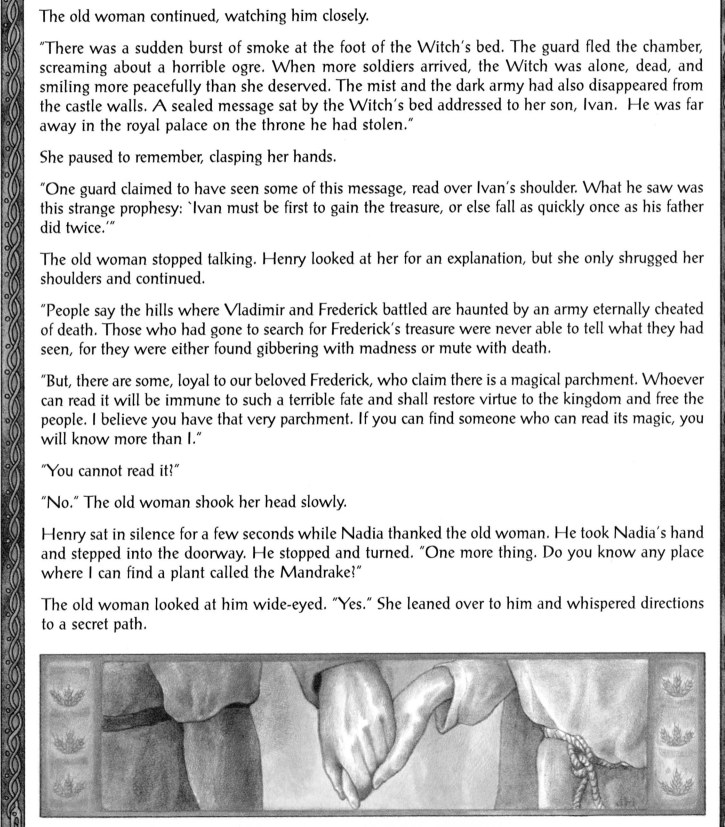

As the couple was leaving the hut, the old woman rushed out of her shack and clutched Henry's cloak with her withered hand. "There is one more prophesy I do not understand. From what I've seen though, you, young man, may understand it. The prophesy says that the true successor cannot kill anyone, any being at all, before he wears the crown, or else a terrible war will destroy all we have."

She nodded and smiled. Henry mulled over her words until Nadia tugged at his sleeve. As they left, Henry concealed a silver coin by a fire pit outside the woman's home. The task was now apparent, but could he do it?

Henry considered the dark, shadowy army in the story and pondered his vision in the hut. He felt certain these forms were created by the sorcery of the Witch. Through his studies, he had learned most creatures spawned by black magic could be destroyed with steel. Some could not be touched by mortals, but neither could they cause harm in return.

There were also creatures of death far more powerful than ghosts.

His vision in the wheat field, was it necromantic ogres as he had thought? Those monstrosities formed by merging a ghost and its mortal remains with black magic! According to fables, such undead creatures were strong enough to tear armored knights apart. They could not be cut by the sharpest sword nor broken by the strongest mace. Only the heaviest metal of all could tear the inhuman hide of such ogres, but even that could not kill them. For that, the legendary Mandrake root was needed. He also had a device purchased from a traveler, and that might be extremely useful.

That afternoon, alone, Henry searched for the root. He carried a small amount of beeswax and some silk cloth. The old woman's directions were clear, but when he reached the special hollow, he saw no unusual plants. Was she wrong about this, and perhaps the entire legend? He searched the ground, the rocks, and the tree trunks, crawling on his hands and knees. Nothing matched his books' descriptions. Maybe I'm in the wrong spot, he thought. He sat down on the edge of the hollow, frustrated, staring at the leafy texture of the hollow. "Mandrake, may I please see you?" he said out loud.

A plant came into view, distinct from the others: the Mandrake.

According to legend, the powerful root releases a terrible thunderclap that could stop the hearts of all nearby when the light of the sun touches it for the first time. He leaned over the plant and wondered if that was only myth. There was no point in taking chances. He shaped the beeswax into ear plugs.

He yelled at a nearby tree. Satisfied he could hear nothing, he grabbed the stalk and pulled. It held fast. He pulled again, leaning back on his heels to add his weight into the tug. Muscles strained in his face and neck.

The plant abruptly jerked out of the earth and, as he fell, the ground shook beneath him. When the vibrations stopped, he unplugged his ears. So, he thought, the thunderclap story was true. Perhaps the other reported powers of this plant were also true. He carefully wrapped the plant and its magical root in silk. Placing it in the horse's pack, Henry realized that part of him wished the root had never left the ground. It would have given him an excuse to quit this adventure.

The Baron stood from the supper table when Henry approached him. He had been told nothing of the results of the trip to the herbalist and was anxious to learn what Henry had discovered. But Henry acted even more nervous than usual.

The Baron led his son to the fireplace in the library. He was proud of this library. Many barons had only one or two books, all preciously handwritten, and he owned more than a handful, plus those he borrowed from other scholars for Henry to read.

"Sit down, son, and tell me what the old woman said."

"It's rather complicated. I apparently have a treasure map, and I'm the only one who can read it."

"A treasure map, all this time and it's only a treasure map? No prophesy, no magic spell or curse, just a map to some coins?"

"It's more than just that. It leads to the entire treasury of a kingdom."

The Baron felt his stomach quiver. "Not the Kingdom of the Necromancer?"

"It's in the Haunted Hills."

The Baron leapt from his seat. His chair fell to the ground with the sound of an ax hitting wood. He paused and pointed to the parchment. "Never! Not that graveyard! I knew that parchment was cursed! You're not going!

"Draw the map out. We'll send some knights to get the treasure. But I will not risk my only child!" He picked up his chair and sat back in it, staring firmly at Henry.

"Father, this is my only chance to earn an inheritance. I could get land from the true king. I know full well that you had to promise the barony to my cousin when you adopted me. Do you want me to spend my life as somebody else's bookkeeper?"

The Baron turned red. He never admitted to Henry that he wouldn't inherit the barony. Ancient law and current diplomacy dictated that someone with true baronial blood receive it.

"There's nothing wrong with keeping books. I know all the stories about those hills. No one comes out."

"This is the key to all my visions. I'm the one who's meant to find this treasure."

The Baron rose to his feet again. "And if you somehow survive long enough to find this treasure, then what?" He searched for any reason that might change Henry's mind. "A civil war next to us!"

Henry shrank back on his chair. "No. I wouldn't start a war. Besides, I would still need to find this should-be king, and prove that he's the real one. I'd sit on the treasure until then."

"Yes," said the Baron, staring at the tapestry, "you of all people *would* sit on it. I still don't see why you have to risk your life for this king."

"I'm not risking my life. I'm the one meant to find it. I know it. It's in my visions."

The Baron leaned back against the wall, eyes closed, massaging his face. He thought: He's a man, now. The parchment is his. If his visions are truly prophetic, I must let him go and follow them. After a minute of silence, he stood straight up.

"I will allow you to go, then. But not alone. I'll send my best knights. And you're to return the moment it gets dangerous."

Henry stared at his hands, then looked up at his father. "No, that won't work. We'd only attract attention from the Necromancer's spies. I need to appear harmless. I'll take Byron, and I promise we'll be careful."

The Baron walked over to feel the tapestry. "Your mother is going to scream when she learns about this."

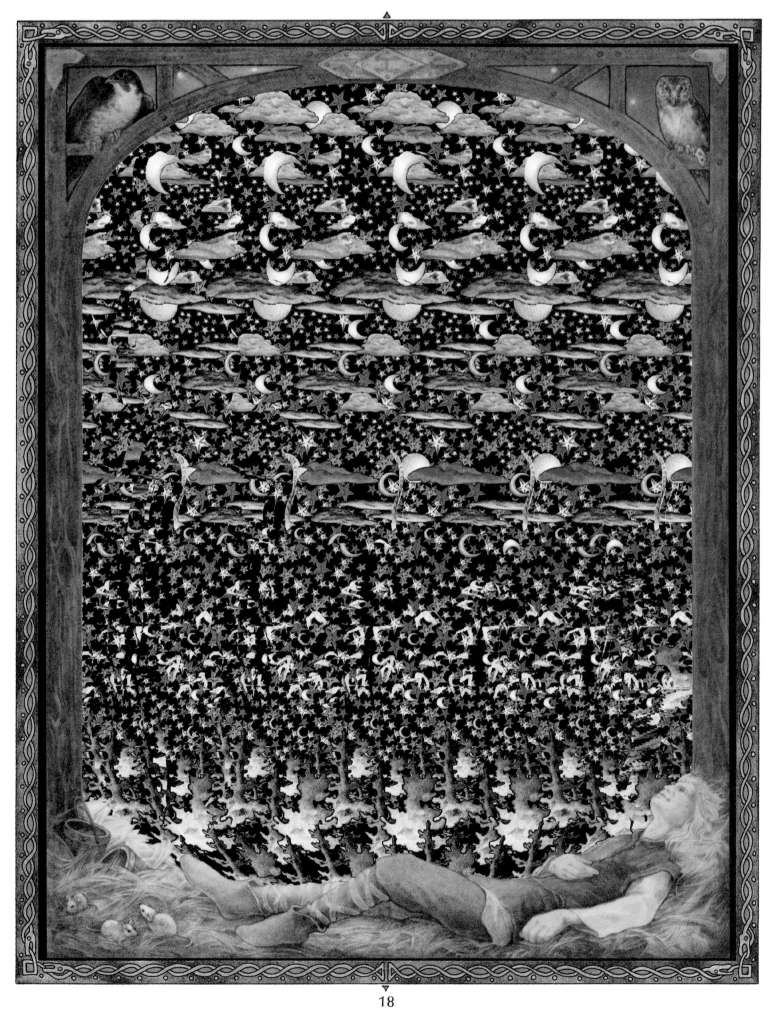

That night, Henry went to the stables to be alone with his thoughts. He gazed up at the patterns of stars shining through the rafters and wondered whether he really was intended for this quest. As he pondered, a vision formed in the clouds and lights of the night sky.

He was stunned. So many different and unusual visions, unlike any he had seen before. It had to mean something.

Byron was excited at the chance for a knightly quest, but he had no equipment of his own. He left to search the castle and came back with a coat lined with plates of cow horn, knee guards of thick leather, a rusty iron "kettle hat" for his head, a small wooden shield, a woodsman's ax, and a hunting spear. He also had some clothing, blankets and rope, and a flagon of strong brandy.

"What are you doing with that?" Henry pointed to the brandy.

A smile peeked through the corner of Byron's mouth. "I found it and felt we should take it," he said, raising his eyebrows. "Maybe we can celebrate when we find that treasure."

"This isn't a party we're going on. Take it back."

"It's only a flagon." Byron stared straight into Henry's eyes as he spoke. "I'm taking it. If you don't want any, don't have any."

"I still don't want it along."

Byron continued packing it. "I don't tell you what to pack. Besides, we may need this, for bribery or something."

Henry looked at Byron's face. It showed the confident training of a knight, the training that Henry didn't have. "All right, Byron. Maybe we could use it."

"What is this *you're* packing? This bag smells terrible, like sulphur, and this other one is extremely heavy. It feels like lead!"

Henry took the bags from Byron and lashed them to a wooden box, the length the same as from elbow to finger and the width of a fist. "They belong to this box. It's something I bought from a traveling Italian soldier. It may be as useful as your brandy." Byron wanted to know more, but Henry wouldn't elaborate. This would probably not be needed after all, thought Henry, so why bring up the issue about whether this was an honorable thing to bring?

Henry also packed the precious root and a large metal needle with a string around its middle, a navigator's needle. When they were ready, they said their good-byes and rode out of the gates of the small castle. Nadia was waiting for them, cloaked and carrying her sling and stones, an oaken staff, a small woolen bag, and a sack of flour.

"Henry, I want to come along. I can ride the spare horse."

"No, it's too dangerous. I want you safe here." Henry dismounted and hugged her.

"I don't want to stay home worrying about you. I'd rather be with you. I can help." She combed her hands through his hair.

Byron interrupted. "We don't need a woman getting in the way. We can't waste time protecting you."

"Protecting me?" Nadia pushed away from Henry and confronted Byron. "I've worked in the hills and forest in all sorts of weather and never had any knights to protect me!" she yelled. "I can handle myself. I've chased off more trouble with my sling than you've ever swung a weapon at!"

Henry stepped between them. "No, Byron's right."

She turned to face him. "I've got a sling and I'm good with it. I've seen Byron's archery. He doesn't have a bow and even if he did, he couldn't hit a cow from five paces." Byron narrowed his eyes at her.

"Besides," she said. "I can cook."

"So can I," Henry said. He tried to ignore a nagging feeling, something important about Nadia. "I'd rather you stay." Henry tried to remember what was bothering him.

"Henry, you don't want to worry about me? You think I want to stay home worrying about you? I'm coming along!"

Byron said, "No, *no* girl is coming along."

Nadia turned away, her fists clenched, but as she stormed away from the castle gate, Henry remembered his vision in the stables.

"Stop, Nadia! Byron, my vision, she has to come with us!"

"What!"

"She has to come with us! I saw it in a vision! She's meant to be with us! Nadia!"

Nadia turned around. Henry took her hand and led her back.

Byron looked at the sky and sighed. "All right," he said. "If you're sure. But we don't need that bag of flour." He rode ahead, muttering something about visions.

"If she wants it, we'll take it." Henry smiled at Nadia. "I wouldn't mind some fresh bread on the trip." Nadia climbed sidesaddle onto the spare horse.

The three adventurers set out heading east to follow a map only Henry could see.

They reached the western border of the Necromancer's kingdom in one day. A border guard with a dirty breastplate came out of the toll house and two other guards staggered out after him, doing up their chain mail vests. The first guard yelled out.

"Halt! What is your name, your purpose, and your destination?"

"We are heading to the market in Tirachia. I am Henry of Veldran, a bookkeeper. This is Byron, my guard, and this is Nadia, my ... servant." Nadia glared back.

The guards slowly walked around them and stopped in front of Byron. The first guard said, "The books you keep don't have much wealth within them, I see."

The other two guards doubled over in laughter, pointing at Byron. The first guard hurriedly ordered them back into the toll house, and the travelers passed through.

Two more days travel took them to the Haunted Hills. Whenever they stopped, Byron gave Henry instructions in basic riding and combat. If Henry could ride, they might at least be able to flee to safety.

After a day had passed, Byron thought his lessons were wasted. He shook his head as Henry picked himself from the ground, again. He wondered if they were really ready for what could come their way.

"Henry, you'd better learn to mount your horse quickly. If we're being chased, we can't wait for you to crawl up the stirrups." He demonstrated one more time. "Here, I'll show you how to jump up. Just grab here and put your toe here, and jump up. Pommel and stirrup. You should be able to do it with one hand, so you can carry a spear or sword in the other." They practiced over and over and over, again.

The next morning, the final purpose of this trip gnawed at Byron. Turning around on his horse, he asked, "Henry, what are we going to do when we find this treasure? Are there any rightful heirs left?"

"I don't really know. I don't even know if we can find any nobles willing to oppose the Necromancer. He's killed so many of them. And I don't think there are any royal exiles. I suppose we could sneak the treasure home and hide it until we find the proper person."

Nadia joined in. "How big is this treasury? Do we need a wagon?"

Byron laughed. "A wagon, yes, a whole wagon. Maybe for the French or Turkish royal treasuries. But certainly not here. We have the donkey. That's more than enough."

Henry interrupted. "I'm still working out that last prophesy. Do we have to find a king who won't fight? Or just remove the Necromancer without a war?"

Nadia said, "What about poison?"

Both men turned in her direction. "Ignorant peasant," said Byron. "Only a coward uses that."

"Well, it's better than being killed and letting the Necromancer get the treasure. Cowardly or not."

"You would think that. But I'm not even going to consider it. I've got honor."

"Do you also have a plan, your honor?"

Byron thought fast. "Everyone knows how useless mercenaries are when the purse is empty. The Necromancer uses Mongols as mercenaries. We'll have the money to buy them off."

"Then our purse would be empty. And there'll still be more of them. Then what?"

"Then … we'll figure that out later." He turned and rode up in front of Henry.

They soon crested a hill from which they could see the Haunted Hills. In the distance, Henry saw the features shown on the mysterious map: the bridge over the river, the mountains, and parts of the road showing through the thick pine forest. As he studied the land where their adventure would really begin, a vision crept out of the forest shadows. It vanished, and he found himself again looking upon the gentle, peaceful countryside. "Is something trying to scare me away?" he murmured.

When they reached the river, Henry stopped. Despite the noon sun, a heavy fog enshrouded the stone bridge that led to the Haunted Hills. Nadia said, "I've never seen a mist that small and dense. It stops only a stone's throw on either side. Fog doesn't do that."

Henry nodded in agreement. Byron rode past her toward the cobblestones of the bridge. "Silly peasant. It's only fog."

Henry called out. "Hold! I see something in that fog!" He paused, "It's warriors ... Mongols, I think."

"I don't see anything," Nadia said, shading her eyes and looking for shadows.

"There's nothing there," said Byron. He spurred his horse on past Nadia. It trotted a few paces, then balked and turned around. "It's spooked, I've got a horse that's terrified of bridges."

Henry said, "It's not the bridge, there's something there. I can see them. My horse won't go near them, either." They dismounted. Nadia fitted a stone into her sling and whipped it into the fog. The stone passed through the mist and skittered on the road near the other end of the bridge. Another one followed and hit nothing but wooden planks. "It went right through that one, shield and all!" Henry said.

"I still see nothing!" Byron laughed and armed himself with his spear and shield. "But I'll spear some cloud for you, Henry." He charged onto the bridge, his footsteps and laughter echoing in the mist. He stopped short, as if he had run into something. Nadia heard him yell and saw his silhouette thrust and slash into empty mist. Nadia turned to Henry, but he had that strange look on his face again.

Nadia ran forward, swinging her staff into the edge of the fog. "There's nothing there, what is Byron do ...?" The staff yanked itself out of her hands and floated into the fog. She reached for it, but something pushed her. Unseen hands of ice pulled her fist over the edge of the bridge. An invisible pole shoved against her stomach and forced her toward the stone railing. Her other hand was yanked over the edge and her head started toward the mist on the river. She screamed. Then a warm hand grabbed her arm. She was pulled out of the mist by Henry, who himself was being pulled by Byron. When they were safely off that horrible bridge, Henry held her shaking body close. Byron was uncut and unbruised, but his shield was in shreds and all that was left of his spear was a broken shaft. He dropped the useless weapons and stomped toward Henry.

"What was that? And why couldn't I fight it?"

Henry frowned. "Ghosts. This land is haunted."

Byron threw his arms up. "You said nothing about ghosts! I was trained to fight mortals!"

Nadia joined in. "They almost threw me off the bridge! They got my staff! My father gave me that staff!"

Henry squeezed her shoulders. "You shouldn't have been on that bridge! You were in danger! Byron is the man-of-arms here. You were supposed to be back with the horses, slinging stones. Remember?"

"How do you hit ghosts with pebbles?" Nadia still shook, but now in anger.

Byron interrupted. "Why didn't you tell us we'd meet ghosts?"

"I did!" Henry's voice rose, and he turned back toward Nadia. "Don't you ever do anything reckless again!"

"Reckless? I was trying to help!" She stared straight into his eyes.

"It was still reckless!"

"I came to help and I will." She pushed him away and walked back to the animals when he called to her.

"Nadia," he said, dropping his gaze to the ground. "I'm sorry. Just be careful." He raised his eyes again, and she nodded.

"What about me?" said Byron.

Henry sighed. "Keep being reckless, you're a knight."

Byron bowed very low. "Thank you, my liege."

Henry ignored Byron. "These ghosts can't cut us with their weapons," he said, half to himself. "But we still can't get through them." He walked to the edge of the bank and looked at the river.

"It's narrow enough to swim or raft here. We'll just bypass the bridge." He looked down into the slowly swirling waters of the river flowing out of the mist. The reflections and plants near the bridge looked odd. He looked carefully, sensing another magical disguise.

"Then again, maybe not." No wonder the ghosts were so eager to throw them into the river. The thing was hiding, not in the water, but disguised as the water itself.

"Do you see it?" He pointed it out to his friends, outlining the head with his fingers.

Byron tried. "Just water. There's nothing there."

"No?" Henry continued to trace the shape with his finger. "Look, it just moved a bit."

Nadia leaned over the bank and said, "I can't see anything either, Henry."

Byron picked up a large, broken branch and threw it at the river. It did not even reach the water's surface before a dreadful head, with teeth like ivory daggers, lunged out and smashed the branch into splinters.

Nadia pointed at the serpent, her voice quivering as she said, "Look at the size of it! Where did it come from? It just popped up out of thin air!"

Byron stared at it, too. "What do we do? How do we get around that thing? We'll have to cross somewhere else."

Vindicated, Henry felt calm. "No, the serpent would follow. We can't fight it. We only have an ax, two knives, and a pot, and who knows how strong that thing is." He rubbed his forehead, thinking. The serpent's head was raised high. Its eyes appeared to study their bodies hungrily.

Byron said, "We'll have to head back. We could bring archers. This place is too dangerous! Ghosts and monsters! We'll need a regiment of priests to get through this evil!"

Henry sat down. "No, there must be a way. Byron, throw another branch."

They watched as the serpent snapped at that branch, and lunged at the stones Byron threw.

"That's something," Henry muttered. "It bites at anything that comes near it."

Then the donkey brayed, and Henry turned toward it. If normal means fail, change the entire approach, he thought. "Wait, I have a plan. We can give the serpent something much too strong for it to handle."

Nadia watched closely and Byron frowned as Henry rose and went to the donkey. He took out the flagon of brandy.

"We'll make a raft for the supplies and tether the horses and donkey together. We'll swim the river."

Byron yelled, "Swim the river? That thing will get us!"

"Not if this works out. Besides, what else can we do but go back home?"

They lashed some small logs together, aware of the serpent's eyes peering over the edge of the bank, watching their every move. The nervous pack animals were tethered together and the raft was loaded with their packages. The curious serpent raised its head higher. Henry carefully tied his wooden box onto the raft and stood up. He felt something cold at the back of his neck and turned away from the river, unknowingly in the direction of Ferdolaf, the capital city of this kingdom. He felt someone was watching.

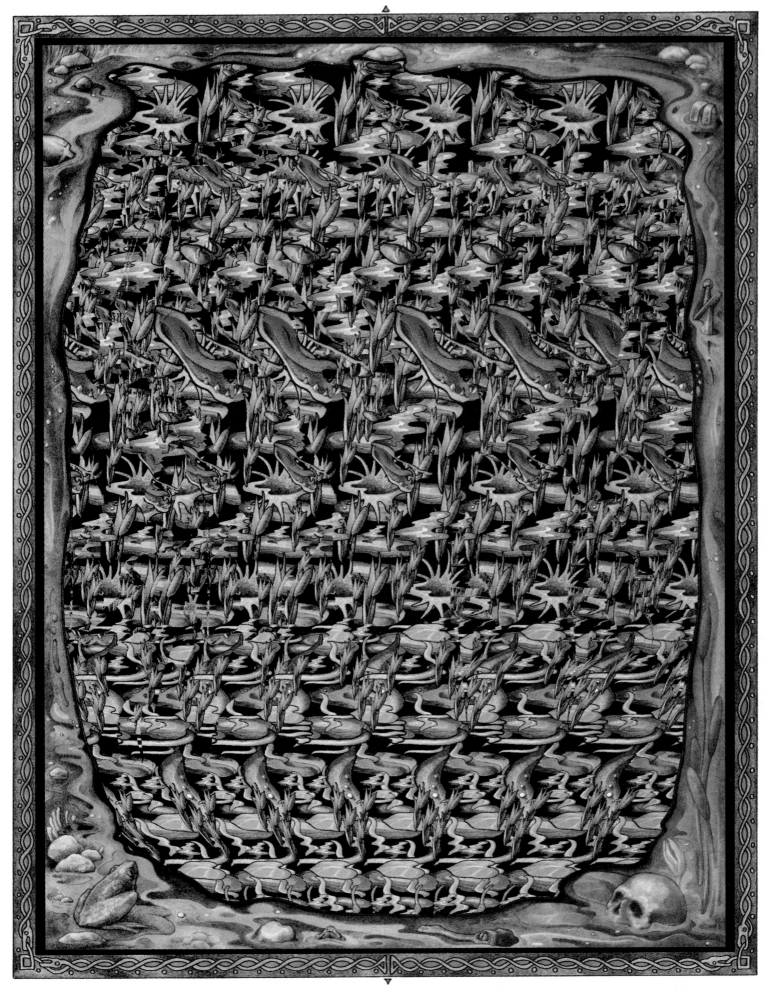

Within the tallest tower of the Royal Palace, two men stared at a massive ball of crystal, watching the magical forms that swam within. Out of those forms swam the shapes and surroundings of the three travelers. The seated man wiped the crystal with the rolled silken sleeve of his tunic.

"Have you ever seen anything so pathetic? Those three peasants won't even last long enough for us to bet who dies first. Look at the stupid expression on that one there."

The large man squinted his eyes and leaned closer to the crystal. His expensive plate armor clanked as he chuckled humorlessly.

"They are indeed a sad looking herd, Your Highness. Should I send troops to kill them if they run?"

Ivan chuckled at the strained expression of his companion. "Yes, but to harvest them, not kill them. We need to stop these would-be thieves, and we might as well use them as a warning to other rogues. Send a small troop of light horsemen and bring the fools back. We might as well have fun protecting our country. We'll have great delight for days, if there's anything left of them. I'll bet five gold sovereigns that only the puny one survives before we catch them."

Ivan let the crystal globe fade into the blackness of the surrounding chamber. He watched the face of his companion frown in the gloom at the thought of risking three months' pay.

The Bull straightened himself. "I think they will all try to run home. But I won't take your bet, my lord. It's too steep for me." Ivan's Champion and Protector of the Realm followed the Necromancer with long, straight, heavy steps. Bikavert, the Bull, was a small-helmed man with massive body plate armor over his great muscles.

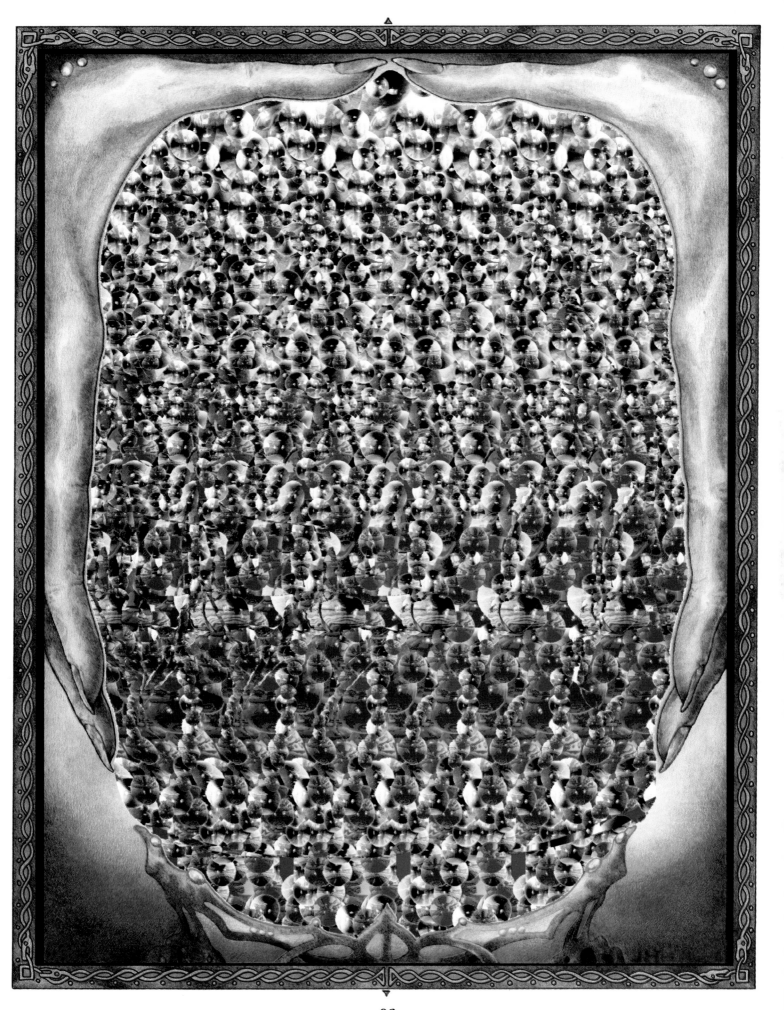

The raft was ready and the horses and donkey were tethered to a tiny tree near the bank's edge. Henry handed the brandy flagon to Byron and yelled loudly. The serpent lifted its massive head even higher to tower over them. Byron grunted and threw the bottle as hard as he could at the serpent. With a swift lunge of its neck, the serpent caught the flagon. After one great, crushing bite, most of the brandy flooded down its throat. They stared at it and it stared back. "Now," said Henry, "we'll see how fast this thing gets drunk."

Byron shook his head. "What a waste, and on a monster like that."

The adventurers slowly moved the raft closer to the water. Suddenly, the serpent slithered up the bank. Its head bolted toward them. They dropped the raft and ran. Byron dove for the uprooted tree the panicky horses were now towing behind them. He and Nadia held the animals back and calmed them. Henry looked at the great beast that waited on the bank. He walked closer to take a look at the monstrosity, ignoring the shouts from his friends, who were still holding the pack animals back.

The creature seemed reptilian to Henry, not wormlike or horse-headed like some river monsters he had read about. Perhaps the creature was created from a snake or from a crocodile, those rumored creatures of the great Nile far to the south and across the sea. This monster seemed to have some intelligence in its eyes. Those eyes were strange and fascinating, hinting of the powerful knowledge required to make such a creature.

He heard a scream from Nadia. He blinked in time to see the serpent's mouth and teeth come at him. He jumped back and rolled. Giant teeth snapped behind him and a steaming breath of sorcery and brandy flooded his nose and mouth. When he got back to his feet, much farther from the river, he saw the thing sitting in the water, still watching them intently. The trio stared at the monster, helpless to do anything but wait.

Soon the creature's giant eyelids began to droop. They waited. A few minutes later, its neck became wobbly, swaying back and forth, and it backed itself against the foggy bridge.

"Now," whispered Henry.

As Byron towed the tiny raft, they swam the narrow river some distance from the bridge and reached the other side just as the serpent swam out and lunged at them. It missed by a wagon length. Henry and Nadia hurried up the muddy bank. Byron led the nervous horses and then pulled the raft on land with Henry.

Away from the river, they tethered the horses and dried their clothes behind separate clumps of trees. When they were ready, Nadia mounted her horse and turned to the others. "Now, how do we get back? We don't have any more brandy!"

They all looked at the serpent and realized that she was right. Ahead of them, Henry could see the shadow-filled mountains emerging behind the pine trees of the low hills.

The Bull's sergeant-at-arms had his men ride hard to arrive at the bridge early.

"Fan out, we don't want to miss anything! Check the bushes as you ride by. You ten, ride ahead and search the banks. You two, go with them and get close to the mist on the bridge and look for bodies. But don't enter that mist!"

But they found no one. The sergeant-at-arms dismounted, walked to the bank, and called out, "Nabhod! Rise up! Nabhod!"

The serpent rose at his command. Its bleary-eyed head swayed widely from side to side. It hiccuped once and slowly dropped beneath the water again. The sergeant's men turned to stare at him, waiting for orders.

"You, return with all haste to our king. We need passage over the bridge. These cursed things are the Necromancer's doings, let him fix them." The sergeant then dismounted and furiously sharpened his weapons as his men waited.

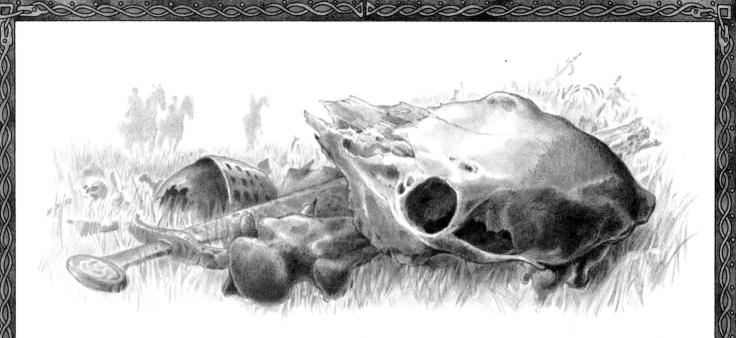

As evening approached, the three adventurers came upon a small plain of scrub grass and lonely trees. The middle of the plain was littered with gray, weathered lumber and broken wagon wheels. When they came closer, Henry saw bleached skeletons lying about in great numbers, surrounded by rusted weapons and armor.

Byron rode up to Henry and asked, "What is this place? It's a charnel house."

Henry studied the field. "It must be the site of Frederick's battle." He pointed over to a little hollow just outside the plain. "We'll camp there for tonight."

Byron waved his arm over the scene. "No! You don't camp next to a battle site! It's wrong! This place could be haunted."

"I'm not sleeping near all these bodies! This place is horrible," Nadia said, shuddering. "I'm going to camp back on the hill there."

Henry turned and faced his companions. "Listen, there is something very important about this location. We're sleeping within earshot of this place."

Nadia pulled her cloak tighter. "We're not sleeping near here!"

Henry hesitated. He remembered his visions before he ever saw the parchment. Some of those visions were about a graveyard that had a tent next to it. He thought for a moment. Then he drew a deep breath and grabbed the donkey's reins, riding to the hollow. "That's my decision, we're camping there!"

He headed for the hollow, and noticed that the others followed well behind. They ate little that evening. In the middle of the night, a terrible sound rose from the plain, startling Henry out of his blanket. Shouted commands, cries of pain, and the clash of weapons washed over the camp. Henry yelled "Do you hear that?" and ran out of the tent.

Byron woke up and stumbled out after him. "What is it? What are you yelling about? I don't hear anything but you."

Nadia peered out of the door. "What's wrong with Henry?" she asked.

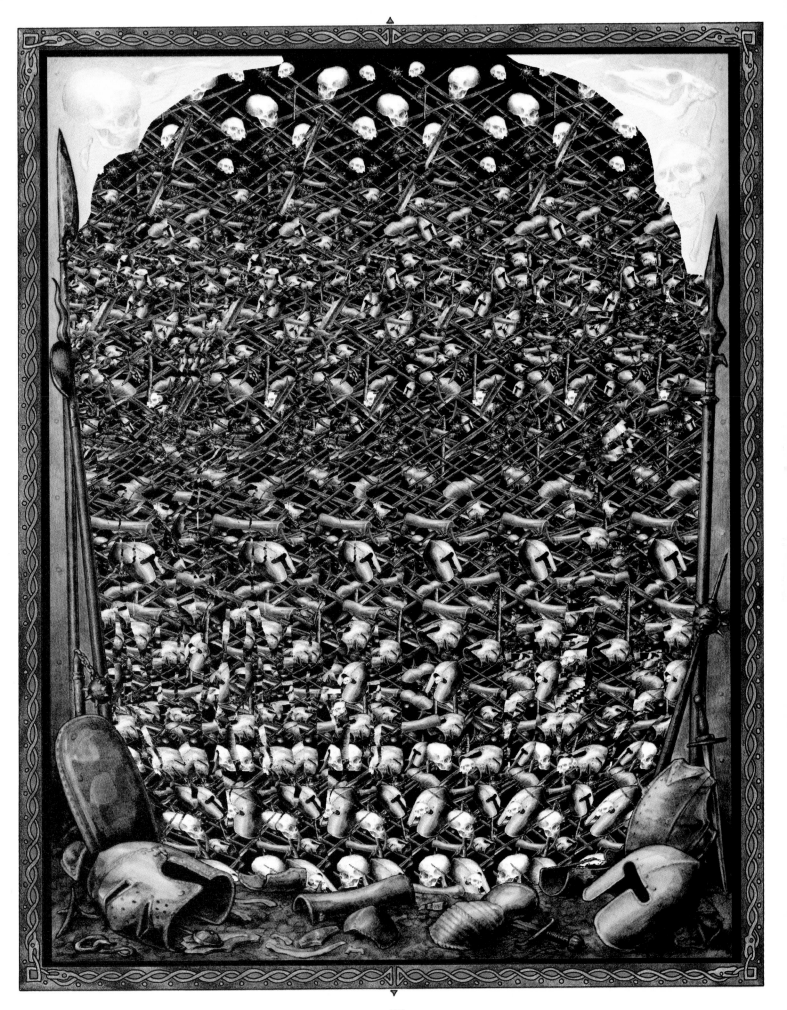

Henry ignored them and ran to the edge of the hollow. He desperately looked out over the plain. In a flash, the night revealed what its magic disguised and Henry saw the cause of the dreadful clamor: a great ghostly battle.

Henry saw an armored man fighting on horseback with foot troops around him. He wore a crown but it fell from his helm. Countless troops fought against them, some in European mail and plate, brandishing long, straight swords, some armored with overlapping rows of plates, with curved Oriental sabers and ornate pole weapons. A giant figure in shining armor, carrying the banner of the Necromancer's family, rode up to the leader and impaled him with a sword, knocking him to the ground.

That must be Duke Vladimir, fighting King Frederick!

Then, Henry noticed Vladimir's suit of armor was empty, and all his troops were empty suits and floating weapons, unlike the weary, chalk-white defenders.

The kingly specter rose from its death spot, turned its pale face to Henry, lifted a great sword in salute, and spoke.

"Search for my sword, take it, and end the exile of the House of Sigismund. Your destiny grants you the gift to see us. Use it, for many dangers lurk unseen."

Henry was shocked. It was the ghost that had haunted him for years, the same armor, sword, and face. This was the same battle of his childhood visions. But not even as a child, waking up crying after his nightmares, did he feel this way. His knees and eyes failed him. He collapsed to the ground, the noise of battle dying in the air.

When he recovered, Nadia was holding him. As he told them his vision, he wondered why the enemy's suits were empty. Where were their souls?

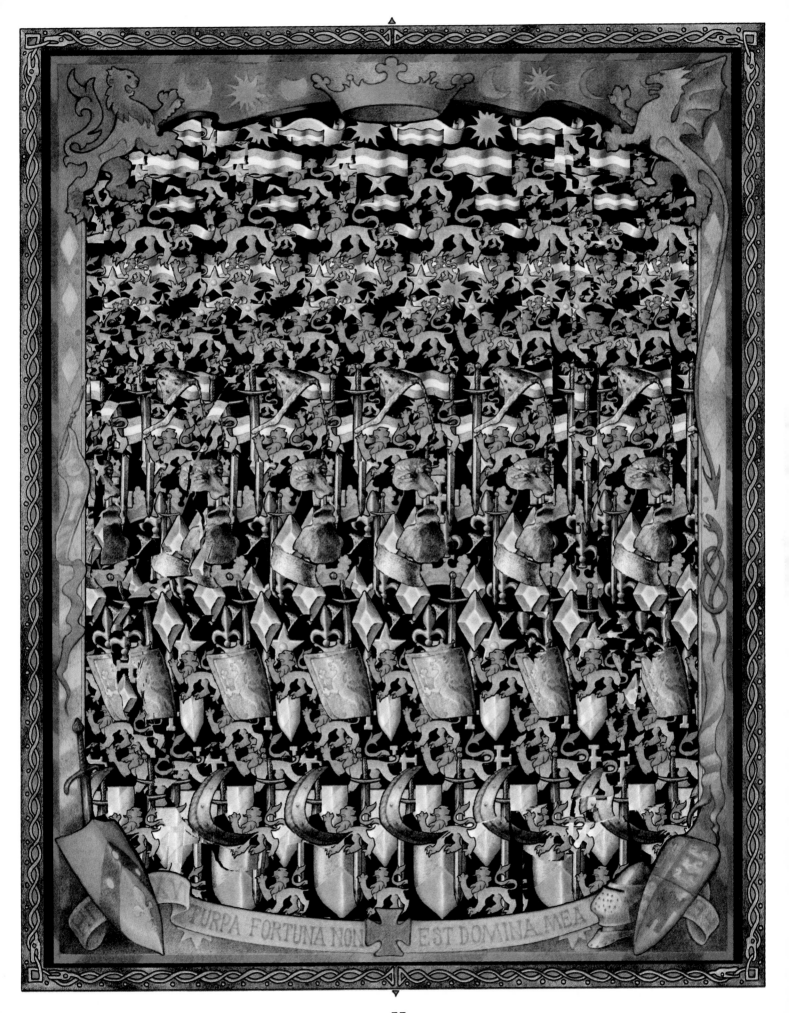

TURPA FORTUNA NON EST DOMINA MEA

Ivan was gazing out of the window when the knight came from the bridge. The knight quickly related the incident about Nabhod.

"What? Really? Fascinating! This will be a very amusing game. Bull, come with us!"

He hurried into his necromantic chamber and sat down, grasping the crystal ball. It started to glow. He concentrated hard, shifting the ball in his hands, until he saw the bridge. He made strange traces on the ball and whispered. Then the ball dimmed.

"There, they can cross the bridge."

"Do you know where these intruders are now, Your Highness?"

The Necromancer leaned forward again, concentrating and tracing on the surface of the ball. Finally, he stopped and drew a deep breath. He frowned.

"Amazing! I don't know where they are yet. But when they do show themselves, my phantom defenders will report …Bull!"

"My liege?" Bull stepped forward with a short bow.

"I want you to leave with a company of knights. You know what to protect. We want no one to escape to tell others our secrets." He stood up and leaned close to the Bull. He whispered through a cupped hand, "Bikavert, do not let them ever get inside that tower. I don't want *him* disturbed."

"Yes, my liege." The two knights turned and departed.

Ivan cradled the crystal ball as he watched the mighty Bull and his troops ride to the hills. This could be so much fun if they're caught alive, he thought. Why let the guardian in the tower have all the pleasure of killing them! Besides, we must leave nothing to chance.

The next morning was bright and warm. Nadia stared at the parchment while Henry packed his horse. When he sat down beside her, she asked him, "Why are you so intent on looking for this treasure if we're only going to hand it over to whoever belongs on the throne?"

"Freedom. If I find this treasure, maybe the ghosts will stop haunting me. And maybe when the real king gets on the throne, there could be some reward. For all of us."

Instead of skirting the battlefield, Henry rode carefully into the middle. The others would not follow. He picked his way through the wreckage and found the spot where the vision spoke to him. He dismounted and dug around some bones, shields, and breastplates, finally finding an object hastily wrapped in an oil cloth.

It *is* here. Someone did manage to hide it, right here during the battle, thought Henry. And Vladimir's men never found it. I wonder who took Sigismund's body away!

He pulled the sword out of its scabbard, wiped it well, and lifted it into the air for his friends to see. It was a battle sword with a long grip. The powerful blade glinted in the morning sun. Henry stared at the magnificent weapon, swinging it's gleaming steel blade slowly through the cool morning air. Byron would like this, he thought, but it's not mine to give. It would be worth quite a lot. But it belongs to the true king, when I find him.

When he returned, he said, "We found one important thing. Now we could return and tell my father what we have learned. We were never expected to find the treasure on this journey. But I'd rather continue on and get this finished. What do you think we should do?"

Byron and Nadia thought for a moment.

"I think we should go further," said Byron. "No one's hunting us and your visions have taken us this far."

Nadia joined in, "If you have all these ghosts waiting on you, you might as well keep going."

Henry nodded.

"Yes, we'll head onward," he said. "There's a key we need to find. What have you got there, Byron?"

"While you were digging, I went looking for equipment. I figure this all belonged to Vladimir's men, so it's not sacrilege to steal it."

Nadia said, "It's disgusting, robbing graves." She turned away.

Byron proudly held up two shields, then an undamaged breast and back plate. He showed steel armor for the lower leg and arm, a shirt of chain mail, and a good helm. He also had a mace and an untarnished Swiss halberd. "Everything else was too rusty, bent, or broken. Or their owners still had their grisly little hands on them."

"I think that's enough for us." Henry looked over the battlefield, abandoned and desolate for so many years.

"When we find the king, we have to get him to bury these poor souls."

Two days of steady travel brought them to the hills. Occasionally, they found abandoned camps of earlier travelers, and less occasionally, what had happened to those travelers.

At every stop, Byron taught Henry more horsemanship, including that wearisome jumping mount. He also demonstrated how to block with a shield and parry with a sword, the basic blows of the sword, how someone would attack him with a mace or staff weapon, and how to duck under the shield to avoid arrows. Henry tried to learn, Byron tried not to swear, and Nadia watched both intently. At least the lessons distracted them and made them feel brave, despite the unknown dangers ahead. And Henry got to laugh whenever Nadia asked obvious questions for which Byron had no answer.

They took another half day to find the cave that held the key. It was as uninviting a place to visit as the plain of battle. Numerous skeletons lay scattered at the cave's mouth, their bones and armor shattered. They stopped some distance away and stared into the cave.

Byron turned to Henry and said, "I see nothing but rock and crystal and old bones. What do you see?"

Henry peered in from a safe distance. He jumped back at what he saw.

"What is it? What did you see?" asked Nadia.

He pointed to the cave. "Trolls, all along the wall. And there's the key. I think the trolls are sleeping." He described the dust-colored, sharp-fanged trolls, pointing to what he said was a key at their feet and to the axes, hammers, and maces lying next to their claws.

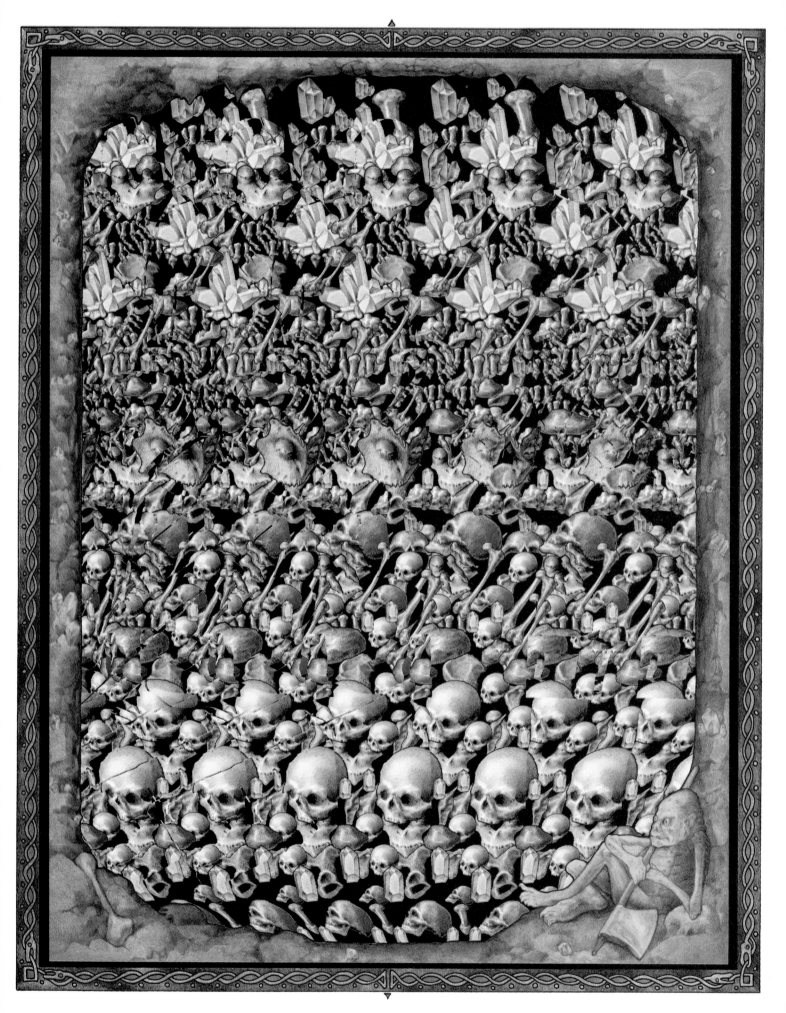

Byron could not see them. Nadia also looked perplexed. Henry stopped pointing and stood there for a while. "I don't know what to do about trolls, do you?"

Byron said, "I know something that might work." His face beamed as he went to the donkey and pulled the bag of flour from the pack. "Before I started squiring, I stayed with my uncle at his flour mill. I remember something he said about flour dust. It may be just what we need."

He cut a slit in the bag and lit a small wax candle. He asked Henry to point out the key again and fixed the position in his mind. Then Byron armored up, taking his newly found mace and the flour bag. Henry took the candle.

Together they crept forward, and Byron wondered what sort of horrible monsters Henry could see. Byron felt ridiculous, in full armor, stalking plain dirty rock, but he could tell that was not what Henry thought. Byron saw Nadia, behind them, ready her sling. She had nothing to aim at either. A rancid stench emanated from the cave.

When they had passed the skeletons, Henry froze and motioned Byron to stop. Henry whispered, "I'm sure I saw some of them open their eyes." He pulled himself to the mouth of the cave and placed the burning candle down. Something unseen made Henry jump in fear and hurry back. He spoke as if afraid of making the slightest noise.

"They saw me, Byron. I saw them reach for their weapons."

"I believe you," whispered Byron, "but I still can't see anything. Do what I do." He scooped his hands into the flour. "Now, throw it into the cave."

They did, filling the mouth of the cave with fine flour dust. Again, they scooped and threw. Henry looked up and said, "They're all armed, every one of them, but they're as stiff as gravestones."

Once again, they scooped and threw. Suddenly, the flour dust in the air caught fire and an explosion filled the cave.

Henry fell back. Byron jumped forward and ran to the cave, seeing monsters fall out from the walls of rock. Nadia screamed out a warning. I know, he thought as he dove into the middle of them, I can see them now and they're ugly.

He bumped strange, wailing creatures out of his way, trying to remember where the key was. Something grabbed onto his back plate and he knocked the creature off with his mace. He saw the key and grabbed it. He spun to miss an ax blow, dodged a groping troll, and plowed through more screaming, stumbling monsters. He felt claws and weapons blindly scrape his armor as he ran out into the sunlight.

Weapons flew wildly by him. He stopped when he thought he was beyond the trolls' throwing range and turned around. He could tell by their eyes that the trolls had regained their sight and senses.

Behind him, Nadia asked, "Why aren't those horrible things charging after us?"

Henry spoke in a firmer voice than before. "They're trolls. They can't go into the sunlight. It burns them. They're trapped in the shadows. They were magically cloaked to hide in the rock. Byron's trick shocked them and broke that spell."

Byron interrupted. "Did you know that before you sent me in?"

"I hoped what I read was correct."

"So nice of you not to warn me that you're relying on some book for your advice. Next time, tell me exactly what I'm up against and what you know about it."

"Next time." Henry shrugged his shoulders and returned to his horse.

When the adventurers remounted their horses, Byron looked at the key: It was covered with dirt and dried mud, but as he cleaned it, he revealed a massive, steel key, plated with gold.

"What's this for?"

Henry said, "I suspect it's the key to the treasury padlock."

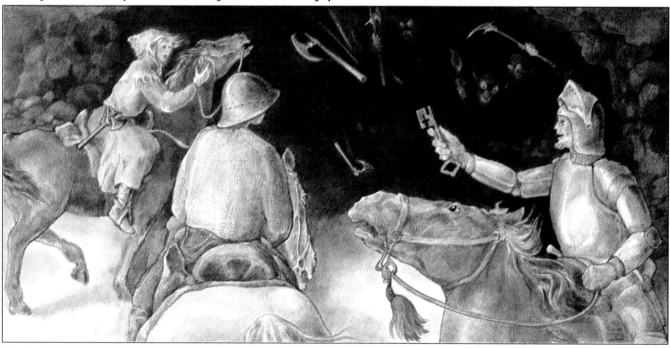

Ivan screamed and raged at the crystal ball. The key! Those witless trolls had the key! Now it's in the hands of those thieving knaves! And they're out of the crystal's range now. He must stop them. That key will be his and they'll pay horribly for this. He smiled with satisfaction.

First, to punish those incompetent trolls. Ivan stared once again into the crystal ball. Dance, dance you blathering fools. Dance out of the cave. He watched the shapes in the ball move reluctantly out of the cave, trying to hold onto the rock or clutching their legs, but unable to stop themselves. They stumbled into the blinding, burning sunlight, where their forms slowly shriveled up, dissolving into vaporous specters. It's a shame, thought Ivan, that I can't hear through this ball, because they make such a hissing when they do that. Great kings should never tolerate imbeciles in their service, living or undead. I need more men like Bull, not the fools around me now.

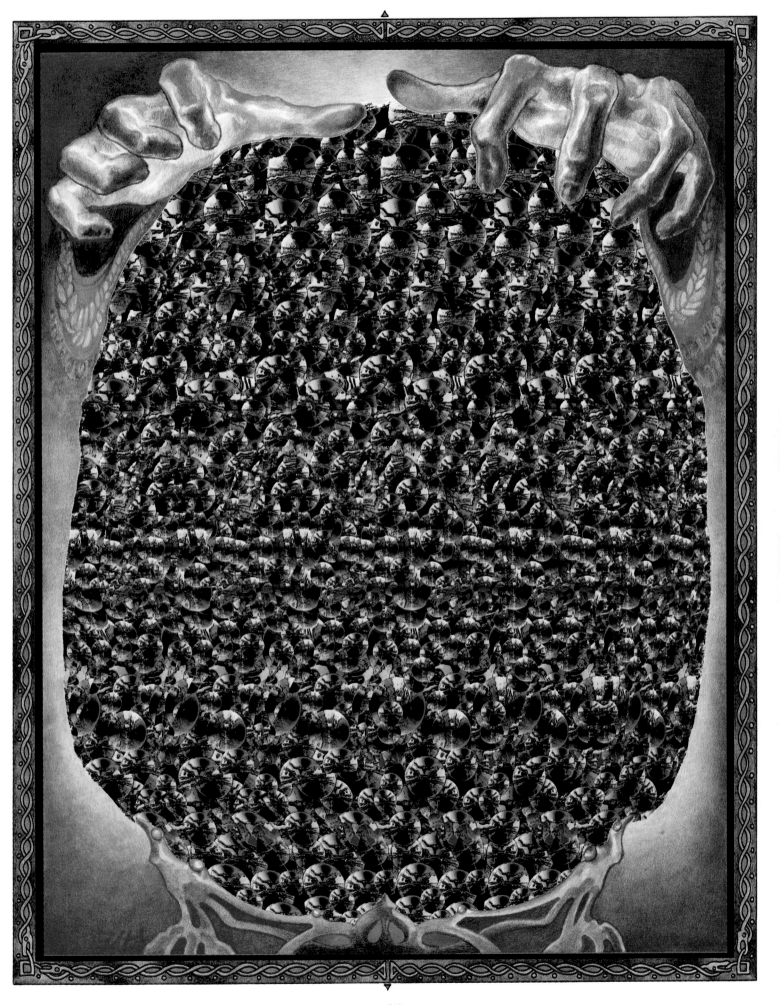

As evening approached, Ivan, the Master of Necromancy, went alone to his dark chamber. "I will crush those peasants myself. I will cripple them and let the Bull drag them back here for finishing. I will throw my entire army at them."

He chuckled at the thought of his great army, all dead, all enslaved, all-powerful, catching those thieves.

"They must not be allowed to reach the tower." He shuddered at the thought of that *thing* in the tower, whose soul was the one link between his present strength and his mother's witchcraft. His mother had warned him. "I cannot fail her. If I must, I will have to go there myself and meet *him* again. But I will not fail her. Curse these thieves! I'll make them scream for hours!"

He read passages from several brass-bound books and made calculations. He went into locked chests of tiny drawers and pulled out several vials and powders to make odd compounds. He took a gold-tipped rod and dipped it into some of the mixtures. Then he drew complex shapes within an ornately patterned circle chiseled into the floor. The Necromancer will be ready when night comes.

He walked into a black, roofless chamber, lined with magical inscriptions of gold. In the center was a chair, richly decorated with the eerie symbols of Necromancy. Two long poles of black and gold spirals were attached to the legs. He sat down in it. He could not avoid this task now. He had to go there.

Ivan wondered if he should have sent troops to that cursed tower to retrieve the treasure. But he knew it would not work. No one could take the treasure by force from that thing, and it would never let anyone but Ivan take the treasure. And Ivan could not face that thing, that brutal, vicious thing, after nearly half a century. Why did his mother have to bring him back! As long as he was in the tower, Ivan could not get the treasure without meeting him. He never wanted that again. But now he had to. Destiny demanded it.

He was right to have the Bull on his way to ambush those peasants, just in case his army of the dark failed. But it never failed him before, and tonight he would marshal all of his haunted troops, every last cursed one of them. And to think his father said he could never do anything right.

The group of adventurers headed toward a misty valley between two mountains, a day's ride away. Near evening, Henry directed them to a forested ravine considerably off the path to their destination.

Henry faced his friends. "It's been too easy."

"Easy? You call this easy?" Nadia stared at him.

"After all we've heard about the Necromancer, why hasn't he tried to catch us?"

Byron leaned on his pommel and looked at Henry. "You think he's going to try now?"

Henry scratched his head. "The map says we're less than a day's ride away from the treasure. He's got to do something now. Remember the old woman's prophesy about Ivan, Nadia? We'll have to be on our guard for the rest of this journey."

"On our guard?" Nadia's eyes widened. "For what?"

"Troops during the day." Henry looked around. "Who knows what during the night."

They dismounted and huddled together to plan. When they were decided, Byron tethered the horses and donkey in the back of the ravine while Nadia took Henry to gather wildflowers. Byron was covering the horses eyes and ears when they returned. When the pack animals were ready for the night, Henry stopped Nadia from starting a fire.

"We'd better not cook tonight," he said. "And don't set up the tent."

"We don't have anything left to cook. Just hardtack and cheese. You dumped the flour." She looked at the sky and turned again toward Henry. "Are we just going to sleep out in our blankets?"

"Yes. Did we get enough flowers?"

Shortly after nightfall, the Necromancer flew into Bull's camp, his litter carried by ghostly whisps. He stepped out of the litter, nodded his head to the knights kneeling before him, and went to the Bull.

"Tell your men to be men. What I do tonight will be terrifying, but they will be safe. In the morning, I will send them to retrieve what's left of the intruders. If things work well, these thieves will still be living."

The Bull saluted, and Ivan returned to his litter. He took his crystal ball from a richly decorated box, inscribed with magical forms. He washed it in liquid from a tiny vial and placed it on top of the box. His special troops had been alerted and instructed, so let them begin the hunt.

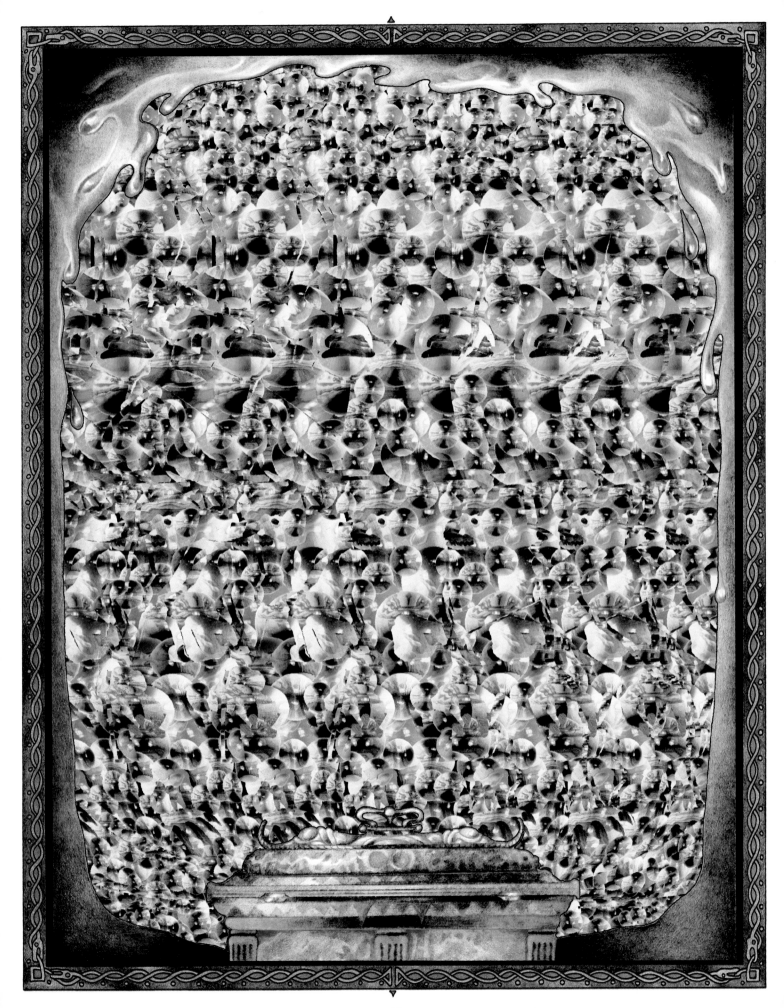

Throughout the cold, moonlit night clouds of vaporous, skeletal ghosts screamed and ranted through the trees, bushes, and meadows. A terrible stench wafted through the air as packs of heavily armed trolls scurried through the grass and scrambled over rocks, grunting and shrieking. The abominations often stopped, frozen in minutes of hideous silence, waiting for the slightest sound or scent to betray their quarry. Then, the nightmare of noise erupted again. As these terrors hunted, mute armored skeletons marched in thick formations down the single valley road. Sharpened staff weapons bounced on their long-dead shoulders, as they tramped the path past the cave, past the road nearest the hidden travelers, on to some ominous distant destination.

The cursed creatures hunted throughout the night, guided, ruthlessly, by Ivan. The longer they searched, the more frantic he became. Still no trace of these thieves, he thought, as he scanned the sky. Was that the morning star's ascending? His troops had combed everything within miles, and, somehow, they had still missed the intruders. They had to be near. He could sense it. They must be crushed, even if he had to find them himself. He ordered his litter into the air, flanked by his netherworld bodyguards. From high above, he saw trolls going into hiding. There were only minutes left. He noticed a ravine. Why haven't we searched there? Yes, those dark objects ... blankets. I've found them! Something whispered in his ear, and he screamed. "No! Not now!"

But he felt his litter turn around and speed back to the camp of his mortal troops. The litter landed, and the specters disappeared into the safety of tree trunks just as the deadly beams of the morning's light touched the ground. He screamed in anger.

He calmed down. His knights were awake and ready. He checked the map rolled next to him, finding the position, and ordered his troops to ride out to the chosen spot. His royal guard stayed behind, lifting his litter and swinging out the specially designed wheels. A team of horses was attached, and the men mounted up to escort him.

The Necromancer fretted over how his army of the night had failed. No horse could withstand the horror of the hunt, nor could any camp fire have been missed. A troll's sense of smell is very strong. How did they hide?

In the sudden peace of the dawn, the exhausted travelers climbed out of their flower-strewn blankets. Byron checked the horses, whose heads were covered with thick cloth and whose muzzles were surrounded by bags filled with flowers.

He returned and said, "You were right, Nadia. They couldn't smell anything either. It's a good thing you thought of the horses, Henry."

"We knew he had trolls, and that they travel only at night. I just didn't think he would have so many." Henry paused and began to open his long box. "And I'm not sure you'll believe what I think is ahead of us."

Byron surveyed the road in the distance. "Try us, Henry. After last night, we'll believe whatever you say."

"I think the treasure is guarded by an ogre."

Nadia's eyes shot heavenward, and Byron raised his arms and yelled.

"Of course! An ogre. And how do we take on this ogre with one sword and one halberd?"

Henry lowered his head and said softly, "You can't hurt this ogre with steel. It's too magical."

Nadia sat on the ground, her face buried in her hands. Byron stood in front of Henry, looking angrier than ever before. He yelled, "You've saved the best for last! What are we going to do? Ask it politely to leave?"

Henry reached into the box. "We'll use this. I brought this weapon for the ogre." It was a short, thick iron tube, open only at one end. A small hole had been punched through near the sealed end. It was strapped to a thick wooden stick that extended past the closed end. A long, thick cord was wrapped around the stick.

"That's the most useless club I've ever seen," said Nadia, peering between her hands.

"It's wizardry," Henry said, smiling weakly. He pulled some lead balls out the heavy bag, each ball partially hollowed out. "Ogres are vulnerable to the basest and heaviest metal of all, as the books say. They are also vulnerable to Mandrake root. It kills them quickly, and I have some." He unwrapped and showed the root.

Nadia leaned forward and asked, "Are you sure it's the right plant?"

"Very sure."

Byron took the tube from Henry. He stuck his finger down the tube.

"If that ugly thing works and we do kill the ogre," Nadia said, "then what?"

"I don't know. I wasn't expecting ghosts to hunt us. It will all work out. I don't know how, but my visions tell me it will." Henry saw the same look on both of the others' faces. He felt sick as he realized how much he had read into his visions. Nobody said anything for a while.

Nadia finally spoke. "We can't go back. We'll get the treasure and hide in the mountains for a while. Let's get going, I don't want to be caught at night in these hills again. And who knows what the Necromancer's got chasing us now."

Henry watched her as she packed, and started packing himself. The weapon did not seem so impressive anymore. Then the three adventurers rode apprehensively over the countless footprints in the dust of the road.

The road was rougher than they expected, and it took much of the day to reach the final destination. On the edge of a great mist, the horses and donkey refused to go any further.

"Henry, we're running out of time. We'll need time just to clear out of here before those monsters come again." Nadia looked up at the sun.

"Let's tether the horses here, off the road. We must be close now."

Henry dismounted and quickly unpacked. "We'll take this." It was the navigator's needle. When suspended on a string, the needle always pointed north. Byron helped him into the chain mail shirt and kettle hat. Henry slung the wooden box over his back. He watched Byron armor himself fully, strapping on both shields and the mace and carrying the halberd. Nadia tucked her hatchet and dagger into the cloth belt of her skirt and he felt even more worried. Then, Byron handed him the regal sword.

"Here," said Byron, "I'm much better at staff weapons than you are."

"But it's the royal sword! What if I lose it?"

Byron stared straight into Henry's eyes. "If you lose it, it probably won't matter anymore."

They entered the mist. Nadia stopped. "Do you hear that? It sounds like marching, in the distance."

Henry checked the parchment and the navigator's needle and headed north. He thought: Could the mist act like night? "Let's get moving fast."

After an hour in thick fog, avoiding the marching sound, they came to an ivy-covered tower. The top soared into the mist. Ruins of a castle wall spread from the sides of the tower, once the gate of a mighty fortification, to disappear into the encroaching fog. Henry led over a drawbridge whose chains had been broken, up to a massive set of iron-reinforced oak doors, barred by chains and a large padlock. No noise escaped from the blackness of the windows, no bird flew from the battlements, and no rat climbed on the stones. Only the mist seemed to move.

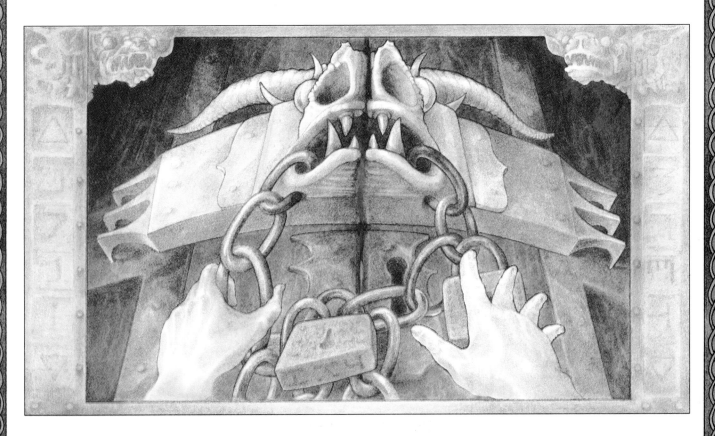

Henry stood at the gates for a few minutes and said, "This is it. This is what we were looking for."

He tried the gold key in the padlock, and it turned effortlessly. The chains fell with a loud rattle and all three of them jumped back. They froze and waited long minutes after the fog had swallowed the clanking echoes. They heard nothing inside.

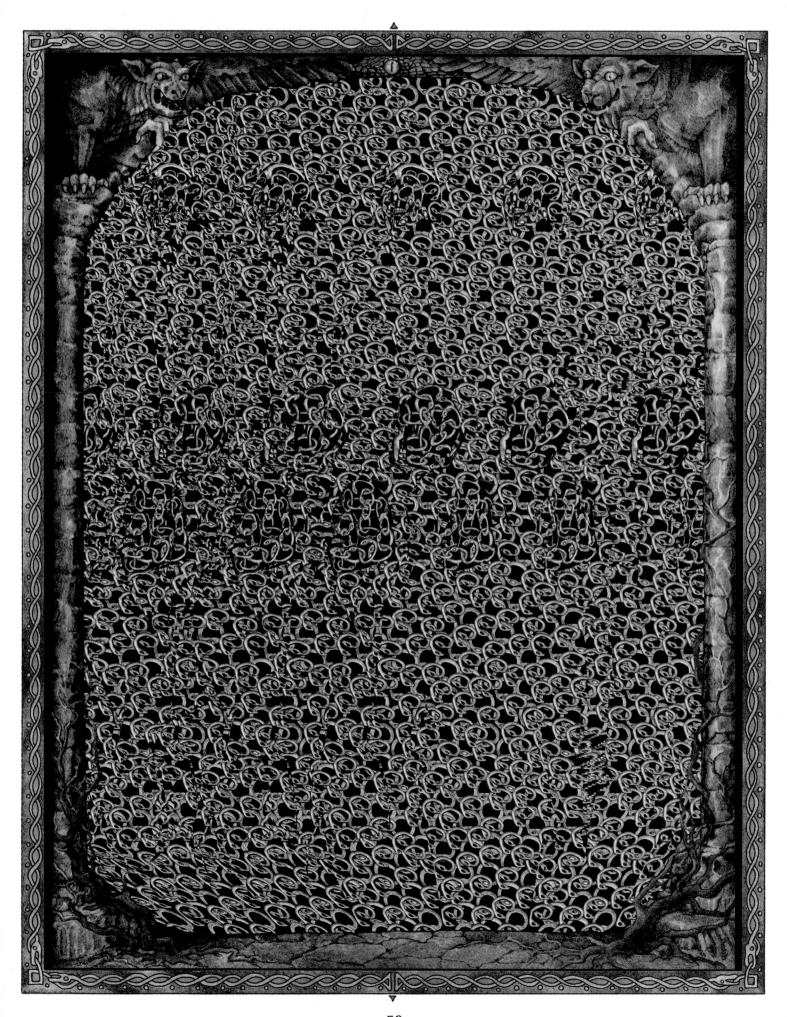

Henry shrugged his shoulders, and they carefully opened the doors. The portcullis was still lifted into the ceiling, and there was no wooden gate at the other end. However, a curtain of chain mail stretched from one wall of the entrance way to the other. Henry stared intently at this, suspecting a trick. The chain mail links shifted and wavered, showing Henry the images of ghostly undead, trapped magically within.

Henry drew the others back with him to make a plan, but heard marching footsteps coming from the fog. He noticed Nadia look in the sky and then to the ivy on the walls. She turned to him and spoke.

"We forgot about the mountains hiding the sun! Those things can travel in the fog! Stay here. I'll climb the walls and try to get into the gate room."

Byron asked, "Why there?"

"So I can drop the gate if we need to."

Henry grabbed her shoulders. "Nadia, you'll fall! Those vines are too weak! And there may be guards up there!"

"So? There's trouble behind us. We can hear them." She broke away from his grip. "Do you want to be outside or inside the castle when they come for us? A peasant like me would rather be inside."

"I agree," said Byron. "We'd be better off inside. But it's still too dangerous for you."

"Both of you are too heavy to climb that ivy, even without armor."

At that, Henry and Byron went silent. The marching grew nearer. Nadia unwrapped her skirt to show thickly woven trousers and strong leather boots. She scrambled toward the battlements. Henry saw the ivy stretch under her weight, but she continued, past empty slits in the walls that were once arrow loops for archers. Finally she was under the outjutting stone battlement. She climbed through a hole that was once used for dropping rocks on attackers.

Below, Henry and Byron heard Nadia's footsteps, followed by the opening of a door. They waited anxiously for several minutes, caught between her disappearance and the ominous tramping behind them. They had to do something.

They entered the castle, closing the heavy doors behind them. The length of wood used to secure the doors was missing, so they used the royal scabbard to bar it. Dim light seeped through holes in the ceiling and glinted off the chain mail curtain in front of them, as they approached.

Still facing ahead, Byron said, "You broke your promise to your father. Let's go." He muttered an oath. Something pushed against the outside door, and the scabbard started to bend. Byron raised his halberd to shatter the curtain.

The chain mail exploded into tiny links. It reformed into a dozen suits of mail, grinning white skulls under their helms, bony hands clutching weapons. Byron swung at one defender. His halberd shattered the chain mail and broke the bare rib cage. It staggered back and readied its weapon again. The rest of the grisly defenders moved forward.

Henry and Byron struck hard. They sheared off two limbs and removed a head. They parried and dodged blows. They were forced back by the bewitched creatures who felt no pain. The headless warrior groped on the floor for its weapon, found its poleax, and slashed blindly, cutting one of its fellows in half.

The two men were now hemmed in against the door. Byron, his arm bleeding, held off several attackers at once. Henry struggled with one, blocking its frequent blows with the two staves of wood left on his shield.

The royal scabbard broke in two and the doors behind them swung open. A terrible reek flowed into the hallway. More undead warriors pulled the great doors wide. Behind them were ranks upon ranks

of their cursed cohorts. Henry glimpsed the hordes behind him.

Byron said, "Pommel, helm, knee, stirrup. Mount!" and the two stepped on top of the knees and grabbed the helms of the two closest guards. They vaulted over the heads of their attackers and crashed onto the ground, dodged the headless skeleton and rolled until they cleared the hallway. The undead turned, and charged. The portcullis gate crashed down. The foremost warrior was cut in half and his legs ran aimlessly in circles near Henry and Byron. Nadia had cut the portcullis rope.

The front troops of undead smashed into the gate and the following ranks rammed into them. One skull was knocked off and it chattered excitedly on the floor.

Henry dodged spears and outstretched bony hands to recover Byron's halberd through the portcullis. Then he saw that his box and the royal sword were being pulled under the gate by bony hands. He hesitated and then dove for the box, grabbed it, and pulled it back. A guard slid a spear through the gate toward Henry. He pushed his feet against the gate and pulled the box free. The spear thrust at him but bounced off the box. He and the box were clear, the sword was lost, and his kettle hat had been trampled into a useless disk. The portcullis gate seemed strong enough, for now. He shuddered and hurried to Byron.

Byron smashed the skeletal legs that kicked him and they passed through a doorway. Here were the stairs to the tower.

"By the way, Henry," said Byron, wrapping a cloth around his hurt arm as he climbed, "you were holding your shield wrong."

Nadia joined them on the second floor, waving an ax shaft. "My ax broke." She looked down through a hole in the floor. "What do we do now?"

Henry hugged her and let go. "I guess we have to hurry and meet that ogre." Beneath them came a steady, dull tramping and the irregular clanging of weapons and armor.

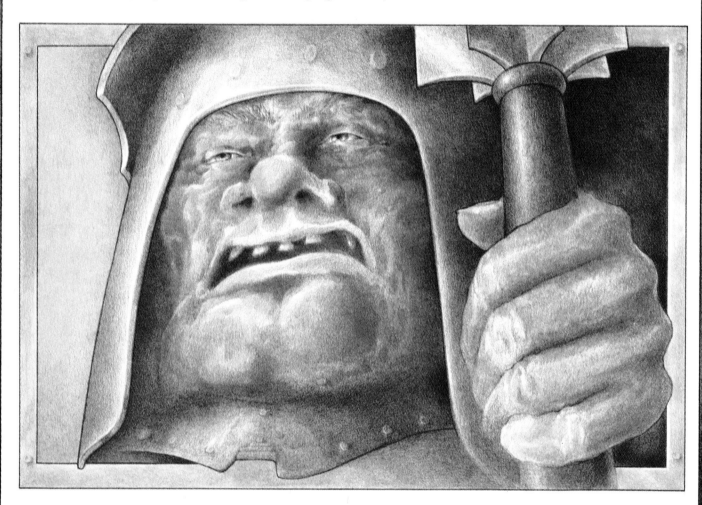

Outside the tower, the Bull looked over his men. The sights and sounds of the unearthly hunt the night before had unnerved the men and some had deserted. Now, they were not eager to go near the castle, seeing the hundreds of undead outside the castle tower gate.

"I want volunteers!" he yelled. Only six stepped forward. Someone shouted from the back, "Get the Necromancer to call off his monsters first!"

"We seven will go to the tower! The rest of you nursemaids can wait for the king to show him what cowards you are!" More men stood up.

A familiar noise in the thick fog caught his attention.

He turned and hailed the Necromancer in his wheeled litter. The king was flanked by his heavily armored personal guard, and undead warriors rode on the litter supports. The driver halted the horses, and the guards lowered the litter off its wheels. While his own men shrank away from the ghastly litter bearers, the Bull approached Ivan.

"Your Highness. We are planning to scale the walls as your sorcerous troops are blocked in the entranceway. The portcullis is down."

"Will a little piece of wood hold us up? Bull, enter through those ramparts there. I will enter the gate room and raise the gate." He stared into the Bull's eyes. "Lord Bikavert, be very careful at the top. *He's* there."

The Bull saw Ivan swallow hard and turn even paler. After all these years, he's finally going through with it, he thought. He saluted and turned away.

The small group of knights walked unwaveringly to the castle, well away from the stomping ranks of the undead. The Bull carried a grappling iron to the walls. He swore vividly and swung the hook in a circle with mighty arms. It flew up to the battlements on a side wall, dragging a rope ladder behind it. The grappling iron caught securely. The Bull climbed up and his men followed one knight at a time, with two-handed swords and poleaxes strapped to their backs.

As he reached the top, the Bull saw Ivan's litter, held by its undead porters, rise in the air, a thick vapor forming under it. The undead hung on, arms stretched, as the litter floated its master over the Bull's own head and flew to the battlements by the gate room. The litter settled down gently on the feet of the porters, and the cloud under it vanished into the mist. One of his knights yelled that the Bull was blocking the way. He climbed over the edge onto the ramparts.

In the distance, he heard more reinforcements ride in, the Mongol captain and his mercenaries. All this for only three fools, he thought.

The Bull stopped. Surely my lord doesn't expect us to have trouble with the ogre. Well, we'll see. And he continued.

Henry and his friends huddled together as they mounted the winding staircase. They passed through a door and barred it behind them. Henry saw the demonic talons and fangs within the walls and ceilings were grotesque carvings and no real threat, but he wondered who or what had the time and strength to cut such things into the stone. Then, they heard the portcullis being raised. Henry leaned against the wall and steadied his legs. Byron grabbed his hand and hurried him on. They ran past another door and reached the top.

They found three doors and a ladder to the battlements at the top. Henry stopped Byron and Nadia and whispered, "The ogre must be in one of these rooms. I'll set up my gun."

"Well, hurry," Nadia said as she readied her sling with some of the lead balls.

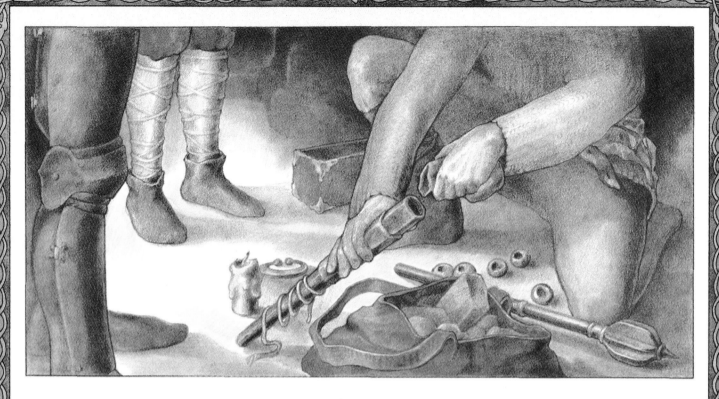

Henry shook half of the black powder from his foul-smelling bag into the tube. He packed a fragment of cloth into the tube, using the end of the mace to press it in.

Byron said, "They'll be at that door soon."

"Then help out. Light this candle. Here's the tinderbox."

As Byron worked to get a spark from the flint stone, Henry took out a lead ball and filled the hollowed-out center with fragments of the Mandrake root. That ball, too, he shoved down the tube, followed by another tiny roll of cloth. He lit one end of the tube's cord with the candle that Byron held.

Henry picked up the gun. He held the smoking cord in one hand and clamped the wood stick against his side with that same arm. His other hand held the tube, pointing it forward. They walked to the furthest door and Byron placed the candle down. Someone pounded on the stairway door they had barred behind them.

They opened the first door and jumped back. There was nothing but more hideous carvings in that room. They caught their breath and tiptoed to the second door. Byron's hand shook as he opened it and Henry tried to steady the gun. Again, nothing but carvings. They hurried to the last door.

"This must be it. Hope that other door holds," said Byron, and he yanked the door open.

Within the third room was a massive oaken chest. Byron and Nadia looked in and sighed, lowering their weapons. "Nothing's guarding it," Byron said. "Wait, I think I hear footsteps, coming from that second door on the stairs. How did anyone get through there!" He turned back.

Henry felt a cold shiver run through his body as he looked in the room.

He saw a monstrous scaly shape, with long, thick arms, a massive chest, short legs, and a gaping mouth, within the stone blocks of the wall.

"The ogre!" Henry shouted.

The thing opened the eyes of its grotesque pointed head and stepped forward out of the stone, revealing itself. Henry heard a gasp from Nadia. He braced his shaking arms closer to his body as he readied his weapon, pointing it at the creature. He touched the cord to the tiny hole in the gun and closed his eyes.

Nothing happened.

He looked at the cord. The dampness had extinguished its fire.

"Curse it. It doesn't work without fire. Get out of here fast!"

They turned and fled. The thing ran after them with powerful strides. Henry ran to the candle, but it had tipped over and was blown out. A crashing noise came from the door below. He worked frantically at the tinderbox, now damp with the ever-present fog. He heard a cry behind him.

The thing had Byron's leg and held him in the air, oblivious to the halberd that slashed it. It grabbed Byron's other leg but then let go of Byron because a two-handed sword had shattered against the monster's neck. Bull's knights had reached the beast's chamber and attacked the ogre. The knight who struck the ogre stared at his broken weapon, then was flung against the far wall, stunned by one massive blow.

The Bull roared, "Stand back, don't attack him. This is no monster. This is Lord Vladimir, once our great baron and the father to our king."

The five knights who were still standing backed away. There was the sound of many footsteps on the stairway.

The Bull slowly approached Vladimir until he was two paces away. He took off his helm and knelt, head bowed.

"Lord Vladimir, I hail you. I am Lord Bikavert, champion of your son, Ivan the Omnipotent. We are here to defend your prize, not to take it. Those peasants are the thieves we are after. We will watch you destroy them and then we will leave you in peace, O great leader of our fathers."

A thunderous voice filled the room and pressed against the ears of the Bull. "You dare claim to help me! Sent by my useless coward of a son! Why has he not come himself? Only he can free me from this wretched grave of a tower. Where is he! He has always failed me! And you dare even talk to me, offering your help, you puny thing?"

Lord Bikavert the Bull tried to say Ivan was now in the tower, but Vladimir was fast. The Bull let out a horrendous shriek as he flew out of the tower window. He landed in a tree, climbed down and, in front of his troops, fled, screaming.

As he ran, someone yelled, "There goes the mighty Bull!" He heard weapons and shields dropping and men shouting to run away, but he didn't look back.

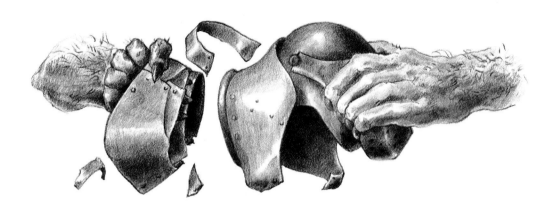

Henry still tried to get the tinderbox relit. Byron and Nadia ran to his side. Vladimir ripped the armor off a terrified knight, after biting his sword in half, and the other knights fled to the stairs. He let the half-armored knight free, turned toward the adventurers, and bellowed again.

The knights had come up the stairs again, moving away from a dozen undead troops. Behind them was Ivan, followed by more undead. Ivan's troops fanned out around the room. Ivan turned wide eyes to Vladimir and spoke softly. "Father? I'm here."

"Yes, he has come, finally! My whelp has some backbone after all!"

Vladimir looked at Ivan and his troops. He straightened up. "You've learned to make armies. I will give you three more to help you carry your treasure."

Henry's fingers were bleeding from the sharp flint as he repeatedly banged it against the steel top of the tinderbox, trying for sparks.

Ivan folded his hands together as the knights kept switching their gazes between father and son. "Father, what then?"

"Then I am free to sleep."

Vladimir turned to the adventurers. He looked at Henry. "You? It cannot be, can it?" His nostrils flared. "Yes, you are!"

Vladimir charged. Nadia slung the handful of lead balls into Vladimir's face. He fell back, and felt the bruises on his forehead. "Lead? You used lead on me!"

Vladimir roared and jumped up in one bound. He leapt upon Nadia, pinning her with one timber-sized leg. His long arm whipped out and grabbed Byron by his helm. But Henry was ready, holding the lit cord and gun.

"Look at me, monster! I will take your crown over your pathetic corpse and give it to the true king! And I will avenge Frederick and Sigismund for the kingdom!"

Vladimir let go of Byron and rose off Nadia to stare at Henry.

"You! You look more like Frederick's wife than like him!"

Henry stared back at Vladimir, as confused as he was frightened.

Vladimir grinned. "And now, Frederick's family ends with you."

"What?"

"You stupid, horse-brained fool! You're the king you're trying to crown! You are Frederick's grandson!"

Henry's mind reeled. He was the heir to the throne? He was the king? His body shook, the cord falling from his hands.

Vladimir lunged.

The gun was knocked from Henry's hand. "Nadia!" he yelled. Vladimir pinned him to the floor with one massive arm. The other grabbed Henry's head.

A glow of fire and a crash of thunder filled the air. The ogre fell off Henry. Henry sat up and saw Vladimir back against one wall, holding his giant chest in surprise. The gun was behind him, smoke drifting from its muzzle. Nadia was flat on her back near Henry, holding the burning match. She looked at him and said, "No one told me it would kick like that."

Vladimir struggled to his feet and gaped at his chest wound. He whimpered and fell to the floor again, shriveling into a dried human skeleton. The Mandrake within the bullet had done its work.

Ivan walked over to the skeleton, staring at it.

From within the tower and without, a loud, almost ecstatic murmur arose and dissipated, followed by the sound of countless dropping bones and weapons.

"Who are you?" said Henry, getting up.

"I am the king, Ivan the Omnipotent! Knights! Kill him, kill them all! Knights, come back here! I order you! Come back!"

Ivan, deserted by the knights, ran to the decayed remains of his troops and grabbed a billhook. He approached Henry, nervously rapping the end of the staff weapon on the floor. "You've killed him! You've killed my father! I'll kill you myself, then!"

Henry and Nadia retreated to the wall. Nadia pointed her dagger at the man. To the side, Byron stood up holding his halberd and walked slowly toward Ivan, gently swinging the blade. Ivan stared at the halberd. He turned and ran.

Byron stopped, still facing toward the stairs, and whispered. "Help me please? My visor's crushed down and I can't see a thing." Henry and Nadia helped him remove the visor. "It's a good thing he was making so much noise. I followed the tapping."

Ivan's personal guard waited on the lower battlements. Ivan had to check his magical crystal first. Strange things were happening now. His father was dead, finally, completely, undeniably dead, and he didn't understand his feelings. Worse, everything was changing without his orders.

The fog had lifted by itself, his undead troops had crumpled, knights disobeyed him, and the Bull was no where to be found. Only his personal guards in the tower and the Mongols on the ground were still here. He lifted the crystal, trying to see what it could tell him.

In his hands, the crystal ball clouded and cracked in half, as if hit by an invisible hammer. It fell to the floor, showing doom in its two halves.

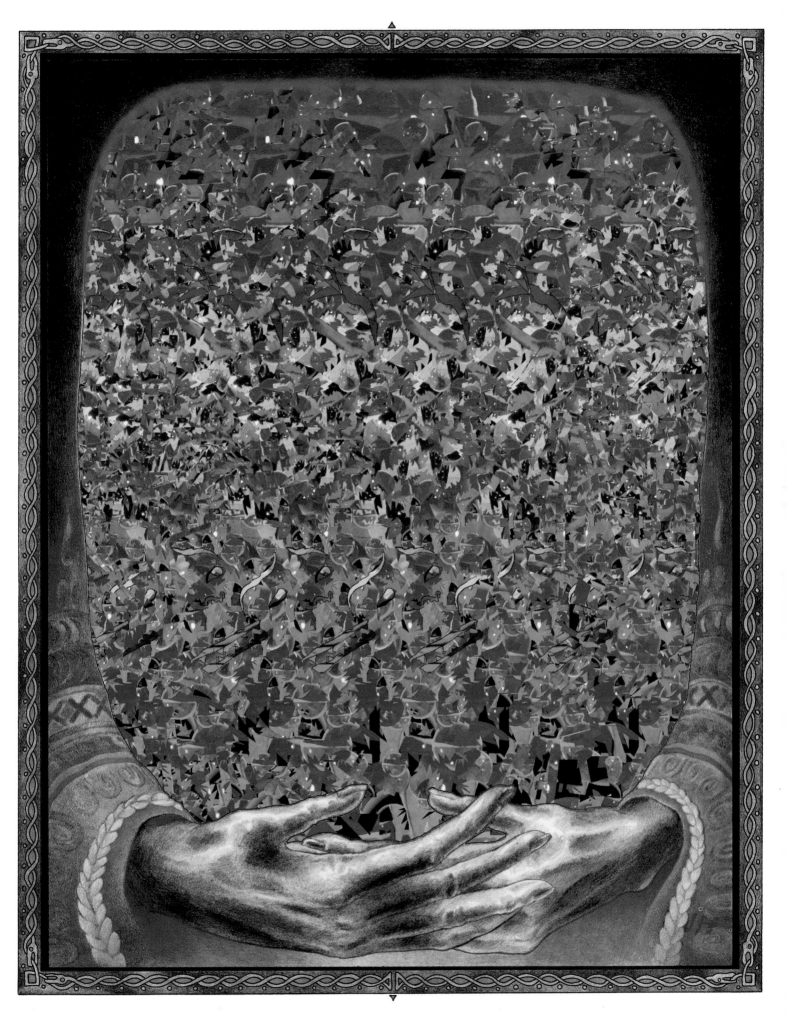

Ivan ran from the fragments back to his guard. He stood at the edge of the battlements in front of the royal guards with their colorful banners and painted shields, relieved to gaze upon his most trusted guardians. But his mind, stripped of its power and its pride, burdened with the memories of years of horror and savagery, turned on its own master. In one terrifying moment, he saw ghosts climbing out of the flags, reaching out of the shields, coming after him. His magic was gone and nothing could save him from the legions of ghosts he had so slowly built up, victim by victim.

He screamed and jumped back, fleeing onto the battlements to avoid their ghostly reach.

"Keep them away from me. Don't let them come back for me! Guards, stop them!"

The guards stepped forward, glancing at each other and at Ivan, holding their shields.

"No, keep away! Keep away from me! Please, stay away!"

Men let go of their banners to step forward. One banner fell close to Ivan. An arm sprang out of it. Ivan gasped. The arm was massive, as massive as his father's arm, and it was reaching for him.

"No, I tried! It's not my fault! Don't hurt me!"

Ivan backed away like a frightened child and lost his balance.

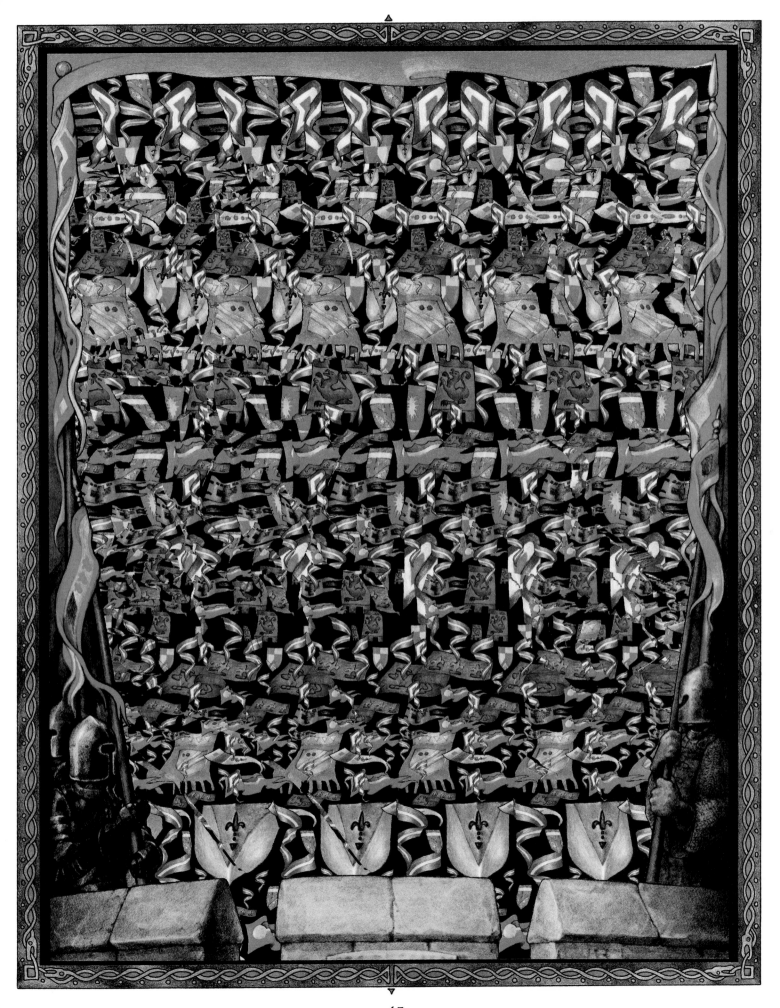

The body of the Most High, Glorious King, Sole General of All Forces and Omnipotent Master of All Necromantic Knowledge made an awful noise when it hit the ground. It lay awkwardly crumpled at the feet of the mercenary commander.

Henry heard the screams. He ran to a window and looked out. On the ground, he saw the Mongol captain staring down at the wreck of a man that was once his employer. He then turned and yelled something about no pay, no king, and something else about taking the royal herds as salary. The captain casually waved his hand, and the most skillful warriors of the kingdom mounted their horses and rode away. Henry returned to his friends.

The adventurers approached the oaken chest. They had no key to the lock, but Byron swung his halberd and smashed it to pieces, jolting the top of the chest open. They all stepped back with a gasp.

Inside glittered the four royal crowns of the kingdom: the golden, emerald encrusted crowns of the reigning couple and the silver crowns for the children. Underneath was the royal seal of steel and silver with its unique insignia, the golden royal staff topped by a ruby and the king's velvet, gold-embroidered cape. And under those were the gold and silver coins of the royal treasury. Henry picked up the king's crown and held it above his head for a moment, then, shaking slightly, he quietly lowered it back into the chest.

Nadia said, "What about the prophesy! If you're the king, you weren't supposed to kill anybody. But you fought your way through the tower."

Henry looked at Nadia. "I didn't have to kill anybody. Every foe I fought was already dead. Very dead."

Byron spoke. "Well, Your Highness, now we take our treasure to Ferdolaf and get you crowned."

"Well said, Sir Byron."

Byron stammered. "I'm not a knight yet."

"You will be when I'm crowned." Byron's eyes widened.

Nadia turned away. "I've got to go home. I don't belong here with you now."

Henry walked to her and grabbed her hand. "What? I don't understand. Why are you leaving? We would have failed without you."

Nadia turned away. "Surviving is peasant stuff. I could handle any of that. But you're a king now and I'm a peasant. I can't be with you anymore."

"I don't care about that," Henry responded. "I love you and I want you to be my wife."

"But you're a king now, not just anybody. The people won't accept me as queen. I can't be a queen."

"I fell in love with you because of your charm and your beauty. Since then, you have proven your-self braver and smarter than any woman I have ever met. You disobeyed my bad judgment and saved our lives in that tower. Now that I will be king, the one woman I expect to think for herself, regardless of what I might say, is my queen. You have proven yourself more worthy than any noble-woman. I will have only you. I've never seen you afraid to try something before: Why are you afraid now?"

Nadia stammered. "But I can't read or write, or do big sums. I can't speak French or Latin. I don't know how to dance or what to say or anything."

"And when I started on this quest, I could hardly stay on a running horse and knew nothing of fighting. We will get tutors for you. Besides, maybe I am half peasant. We'll both learn what we need."

"I love you too, Henry." She stepped into his embrace.

Bull's knights peered out of the stairway and then climbed up. They saw the open chest and its contents.

With that, one of the knights strode to the chest and lifted up the crown of the king. He walked to Henry and placed the crown on his head. Then he drew his sword, knelt, and pointed it at Henry's heart. Nadia gasped. The other knights did the same. Henry was concerned, for he had five blades facing him. Then he remembered reading about this ritual.

"I accept your oath of fealty." The swords were resheathed, never again to be drawn against Henry. The royal guards soon swore their oaths, as well.

Henry and his friends searched for and found the royal sword and set fire to the castle tower.

The souls of the undead, no longer enslaved, were free. Their motionless mortal remains lay strewn about, leading away from the gate in a long, wide carpet of rusty armor, rotten wood, and gleaming bone that shone in the twilight. There would be no hunting army of trolls tonight, or ever again.

And thus the kingdom prospered, safe from war and ruled by a shrewd but honest royal couple, as anyone with vision could foresee.

About 3D Images

The 3D effect has been described in science journals for years, even as early as the mid-1800s where the phenomenon was described as "the Wallpaper Effect." Optical researchers have been working with such images for decades, studying how the human eye works. They coined the term "autostereograms." No special viewing tools are required to see autostereograms, unlike other 3-dimensional illusion processes (which require special glasses or viewers).

The process works by repeating regular patterns of randomly placed objects (often called "pixels," after the pixels on a television screen). Through a sophisticated computer process, some of these pixels are then rearranged, creating a horizontal displacement. Because the pattern seems to repeat regularly, the brain erroneously interprets separate pixels in the same horizontal line as being part of the same spot on an object. Then each eye notices the different angle it requires to focus on that part of this imaginary object, and interprets the difference as an effect of depth.

How to See the 3D Images

For beginners, the image is easiest to see if the picture is viewed through shiny clear plastic or glass. Look through the picture by focusing only on a reflection in the shiny covering. The reflection of a light behind you, or even your own reflection, will do. Look at the reflection, then shift your concentration to the picture without changing the focus of your eyes.

Do not focus on the picture. Relax your eyes. It may take a few minutes at first, but once you have seen the image, it gets much easier and much faster (e.g., seconds) to see it again.

If the above method does not work, then you can try this method:

Move the picture up to within a few inches of your eyes and find two similar but distinct points about two inches apart on the paper. Place your nose between these two points so that each eye is over one of the points. You should be able to focus your eyes in such a way that the two dots appear as one single dot.

Slowly move the book away while concentrating on seeing the two dots as one. Shift your concentration from the dots to the picture.

It helps to be patient and relaxed. The image will not come out if you try to force it. Don't be discouraged if you don't see it the first time you try, as most people take more than one try!

Page 6

Page 9

Page 12

Page 15

Page 18

Page 23

Page 25

Page 27

Page 29

Page 33

Page 35

Page 37

Page 40

Page 43

Page 46

Page 50

Page 57

Page 61

Page 63

Page 67